AF583279

HATCHIE

KEEPER OF THE SECRET

ED "DOC" HOLLIDAY

Hatchie: *Keeper of the Secret*

Ed "Doc" Holliday

Published by:
Mainstreet Books

Book Design: Linda Lanning

Printed in USA by The Print Steward.

I dedicate this book to my wonderful wife, Leslie. Through the years, the joys, and even the tears, you help make every day new again. Love you always.

COMING SOON!

Please continue to check hatchiebooks.com for new information on the release of the next book in the Hatchie series coming 2023!

SOUTH
ATLANTIC
OCEAN

Chapter 1

Like a touch of honey on golden leaves glistening, the early morning sun revealed the hint of moisture surrounding the drying gold leaves on the trees. The leaves were yellowed, not by the changing of the seasons but by the heat and lack of rain, causing the very edges of the leaves to crinkle with a dead brown observed up close. The summer stilted tops of the yellow poplars were standing gracefully across the Hatchie Hills rolling up from the Hatchie River. The river itself meanders through the Hatchie Bottom that visually flattened for a mile with its late season crops now growing in its rich dark soil. The hills themselves were made of red dirt atop of clay. The gullies and ravines throughout these hills showed mostly the red dirt, but sometimes the clay beneath was seen, too. Patrick's eyes darted from the honey-dipped yellow poplar leaves to the river itself where the morning's light caught the last of the fog coming off its banks. The coolest, most visual, and bird-chirping sounding part of the 24-hour cycle in the summer seemed to be always that reprieve just after the crack of dawn.

Patrick gripped the door handle of the well-used truck that was fitted to haul small stick pulpwood. His grandfather drove the truck with both hands manhandling its obtrusive mechanical nature. His grandfather wasn't a large man, and his thin frame was almost comical in the big truck. Patrick looked down to the floorboard and the middle-positioned gear shaft where he could see through the floorboard and watch the blacktop from inside the cab. "Pappy, I don't know why we had to get up so early today. I told you that I could work all day if you need me to," Patrick shouted above the engine's clatter.

His grandfather looked over and shouted back over the loud motor, "It's because what we don't get today, we may not be able to get until next summer. The gully area is just now dry enough to get this truck down in there and back out with a load of wood. If it rains again, it may not get dry enough before you go back to college and who knows? In a year you may not be back to help me."

"Maybe not," Patrick hollered back as he thought about that scholarship for European study abroad that he had applied for.

Neither said anything as quietness settled like a thick fog for a while. The trees were exhibiting the full brunt of the Mississippi heat. The dry weather had caused the leaves of the hardwoods to start falling as if it were early autumn. Just a month before, the leaves were in their full glory, green sheer-spiritedness, bright and cheerful-like. And just a month or so before that, they had been buds in spring with blooms and pollen and in a magic season of birth and beauty. Now like aging children growing fast into adulthood, the leaves were heat-thrusted into a midlife crisis---some falling off the tree like the world thinning out class reunions a little at a time. But after middle age the numbers start accelerating, the dropping leaves increasing into autumn and the increasing of the dropping leaves continues until only the few make it into the late winter season. But all the leaves will be gone before the spring comes again. Patrick thought about the leaves and life and how the leaves were like friends he knew and classmates and communities and then it struck him. He reflected from his boyhood years and could see through his young boy eyes his Pappy saying:

"You see, the Chickasaws were great warriors. Now you can remember the warriors like watching leaves on trees. The young warriors were like buds when they were training and then were full grown, and some would die in battle like leaves coming off the trees in the summer. In big battles they might fall like a mighty wind blowing, but one day, no matter how great a warrior they were, all would one day return to the ground. That is why they would fight every battle as if it was a great day to die!"

Patrick looked over toward the profiled face of his grandfather, and in his memories he returned to Pappy's storytelling. "Oh, but don't forget the evergreens—their leaves don't fall. And there once lived this old Chickasaw medicine man who was like the evergreens because there was always a medicine man. But I never knew him. I thought that I knew him because the Judge knew him better than anyone before the old medicine man died. The Judge knew this land. His great-grandfather purchased the land from a land dealer who broke up pieces of his company's purchase from the government after the Treaty of Pontotoc in the 1830's. The Chickasaws were never defeated. The Judge always said they were never defeated but were roughened up by the slave trade. The chiefs all thought they needed to imitate the rich white settlers in other regions, so they started acquiring slaves; then other Chickasaws wanted slaves, and then they wanted the slaves to do all the things that they had been doing. Then they just lost their edge in life so to speak. But Tippahjo was the last medicine man in these Chickasaw lands. He never left. He was a young teenage warrior when the first movement to Oklahoma started. A lot of the Chickasaw didn't want to leave their lands. Therefore, many of them stayed until the U.S. government pretty much told everyone that all Chickasaw families had to vacate, yet a handful still stayed. Of course, some had married white men, and even a few warriors had married white women. The warriors had to take their white women to Oklahoma, but the Chickasaw women could stay with their white men on the land here. And in some cases, the Chickasaw women married black slaves who were then liberated by the tribe. And some of the black women married Chickasaw warriors, and they mostly ended up in Oklahoma. Some of these families stayed, and some were forced to move to

Oklahoma. The government didn't want Indian stragglers hanging around, but a few stayed on to help the settlers and farmers with working the land. Tippahjo, now he was their medicine man's son, and he was in his early 20's in the 1840s. His father, the medicine man, now, he went to Oklahoma because he felt obligated to the tribe. But he wanted his son to stay, and his son, Tippahjo, lived to be almost a hundred the Judge said. The Judge was born in 1898, and Tippahjo taught him all the Chickasaw ways: to hunt and fish and to read the seasons and even taught him to do a rain dance. He apprenticed him like he would have trained the next medicine man as he was trained."

Patrick continued to stare at the profile of his grandfather and then asked, "Pappy, why do you suppose Tippahjo stayed on the land here?"

His grandfather took his eyes off the road and looked right into Patrick's blue eyes and said, "I know but I'm not sure you would understand."

"Why not?"

"Well, let me just say that Tippahjo had a secret."

"What kind of secret?"

"Tippahjo told the judge something that he told to never tell anyone until he was led to tell one person and then never tell anyone else. Tippahjo was the Keeper of the Secret."

"What does that mean?"

"Well, that's a long story, I'll have to tell you sometime when I'm not shouting over this loud engine."

The engine was rattling louder because the old log truck had left the paved road and was now shaking and bumping down a dusty gravel road with red dirt dust rising and the green vines and limbs near the road were crusted over with a thick layer of dirt dust leaving all things near the road with an earthen red tint. Patrick could even see the red dust now coming up the hole in the floorboard. Soon they traveled to a gate made from three barbed wires with a small cedar pole in the middle and a wire hook to fasten to another cedar stick post as the gate to keep the cows in the pasture. Patrick unhooked the gate; and as the truck pulled through the gap, he refastened the gate and ran to catch up to jump back in the cab of the truck.

Now was the fun part of the truck ride. Three years before, Patrick had visited a cousin in California, and his cousin's parents took them to Disneyland. And there he rode the Indiana Jones ride over and over. His cousin and he did the single rider line and rode it more than ten times each. And as the ride jerked and scooted the riders back and forth in their seats, Patrick had decided the log truck ride over the dirt field roads through the pine trees and over water ditches was even more fun than the Indiana Jones ride---especially on muddy days. But today was not muddy. Patrick's grandfather had struck a deal with the Judge's son to clear out the scrappy pine trees as pulpwood. He would thin out these pines so that the better ones would grow into even bigger sawlogs, and the Judge's son would have improved and more valuable timberland. Patrick's grandfather would take the small stick pulpwood to market and keep all he made; and when Patrick helped him, he was giving Patrick half of the money to help pay for his college. The Judge's son called it a win/win/win situation.

Patrick's grandfather had grown up on the land just as the Judge had. As a boy, his grandfather's father had sharecropped the Judge's land, and as a boy the Judge instilled in Patrick's grandfather the same Chickasaw traditions that Tippahjo had instilled in the Judge. In fact, the grandfather had planted many of the pine trees that he was now thinning out for the Judge's son. The land had been cleared for farming over the first two generations of the Judge's family. The Judge had learned as a small boy how the red-dirt pioneers of his ancestors had hitched mules to the large stumps to help clear the land to plant crops. He was told about how the biggest stumps from the virgin forest often were plowed around for years and in some cases decades before they finally rotted out enough to be pulled from the earth. As agricultural methods improved, so did the pioneers increase their desire for more farmable land. But the Hatchie River was the untamed god of spring which would rise to swallow many a crop and dash the hopes and hard work of many a farmer until FDR's Depression-era government programs provided funds to have the channels contributing to the river engineered by man to keep the Hatchie within its banks for the most part. Still though, like its destination the "Father of Waters" it can never be fully expected to stay within its borders. Like the Mississippi itself, man can plan but cannot contain waters when God decides for the cup to "runneth over."

The Hatchie River and the land tangled together in a slow dance of nature and vision. Flawlessly the hills rolled up from the bottom land that had been flattened out by hundreds of years of spring waters rushing and swelling the riverbed until the hills gave enough of themselves to mix with the dead leaves and debris to fill out the flat bottomland. Within the hills were the little streams trickling down from the crevices and gullies; the many looping rounds of hills would drop off into the Hatchie Bottom that extended along the river. Sometimes there were quicksand and dark murky swamplands. Dense cypress trees with their mystic knees rising from stagnant waters that would at times cause a blue flame seen at night by coon hunters who showed no fear in tempting the spirits of the Hatchie Bottom. What was beautiful in the day could be treacherous and deadly in the night---just as where there is goodness, there evil lurks to oppress and attempt to overcome the good. The chorus of night sounds from the crickets, cicadas, owls, bobcats, and a canopy of creatures made these regions notorious for sightings from Bigfoot to black panthers. As daunting as the night in the murky swamps of the Hatchie River can be, the mornings give light on a roughhewn beauty carved from the very beginnings of what becomes the Appalachian Mountains. The initial foothills are like scattered steppingstones splattered on the earth just before the Appalachians start growing their many peaks all the way into the Northeast states. All the trails in the Appalachians can be tied back to these foothills where the original Natchez Trace once pierced the birth of the Hatchie as if it were the heart of a living system, beating and pushing life flooding through a region affluent with a delicate edge of living plants and creatures.

The beaten-up log truck rattled to a stop. Both Patrick and Pappy opened their doors and stepped onto the light dew on the forest floor. Pappy lifted his chainsaw and then planted it down as the sound of metal hitting metal rang into the quiet woods when the saw landed onto one of two steel bars extending behind the cab of the truck. Pappy said, "It's early in the morning to try and remember a lot of things in a big story." Patrick looked over at Pappy, and with his eyes he silently but effectively nodded his head to mean go on. "So, you want to know Tippahjo's secret." Patrick looked toward Pappy nodding his head more deeply for yes. "There never has been a land like the land here. The Chickasaw knew that, and they had a secret. They still have that secret that only one person knows about now."

"What's the secret?"

"I know about where it is, but I really don't know what it is."

"You know it?"

"Yep."

"Is it treasure?"

"I told you that I don't know for sure. I've never seen it. Judge says the best he figured it that ole Hernando DeSoto was high near to sniffing it out, but the Chickasaws, well, they snookered him and pushed him on to see the Mississippi River." His grandfather smiled and then said, "I knew when I read the textbooks about DeSoto discovering the Mississippi River that the Judge had already told me that the Indians from around here would just laugh when they ever heard that story. The Mississippi River was discovered before the Chickasaw. And the people who discovered the Mississippi used it. They were here long before the Chickasaw because the Chickasaw came and found the people who kept the secret, and they became fierce warriors to make sure the secret was kept."

"What's the secret?"

"I told you that I have not seen it."

"But you know the secret."

"The Judge told me to tell only one person just as he was told to tell only one."

"Well, have you told that one person?"

"You know these woods and this land better than anyone else I know. I taught you where to hunt and as we have crisscrossed these hills and bottoms, so you have felt its heartbeat."

"I have, haven't I?"

"You have."

"I've never thought about it like a breathing thing. This land, this river, this whole of earth squeezed and wringed beneath sky and water. I've never thought about the Hatchie Bottom being beautiful except when maybe the dogwoods bloom in the spring or all the bright leaves on the hills in the fall, but now that you have mentioned it, this land is unlike any other. I have stood in the Smoky Mountains, and I've seen the Rockies; but in all their majesty, they cannot pull my breath deeper to feel such a life force and move within me like this land does."

"Son, hidden in these hills lies what Hernando DeSoto wanted and what Ponce De Leon looked for, too."

"You mean the fountain of youth?"

"I don't know the whole story about that, but the Judge said that it was here, too."

"Where is here?"

"We are in the heart of it right here, I'm telling you. You wanted to know why we only come deep into the heart of this land in the summer. It is because this deep heart is not kind to a log truck with a full load of pulpwood. It stays wet down here, and with the deep forest floor of hardwoods mixed with these pines, the ground hardly ever gets to completely dry out but for a couple of weeks in the later summer. But the secret is here."

"Where?"

"Well, it's down in there," his grandfather said pointing to a drop in the tree level from the ridge on which the truck was parked. I was going to get this saw sharpened before we go down into the drop off and then right next to that deep gully. The gully wasn't there in the Chickasaw days, I wouldn't think. Judge said the deep gully was because too many trees were cut down and the hills caused the water to flow too fast and then these deep gullies were ripped into the land, ripped across the hills where once shallow dips existed and became the deep gullies of today. Judge said Tippahjo told him that the land was eroding away because the white man did not know how to care for it. He knew the Hatchie flowed north to empty into the Father of Waters; and as the farmers plowed more land and the erosion washed more topsoil away, that red dirt from the hills ended up in the Gulf of Mexico. Funny, though, Judge said that Tippahjo never called it the Gulf of Mexico; he called it River Sea. He said the Indians believed all the waters of the world rolled into that sea including the land beyond the sea."

"You mean where the white man came from? He believed that the rivers of that land flowed into the Gulf of Mexico. Technically he got it right, didn't he?

"Well, I remember questioning the Judge about that. Then the Judge went into the craziest story that I had ever heard about the Bible and the Hatchie Hills."

"You mean about those traveling preachers holding that revival for the Chickasaws? I remember something about that sometime before President Jackson had them removed with the Trail of Tears episode."

"No, I mean verses in the Bible that the Judge said were about the Hatchie Hills?"

"You've never told me anything about that, Pappy."

"No, I haven't. It's part of the secret."

"Well tell me, now."

"It's not that simple."

"Why not?"

"Well, it's a long story and we must get to work. Maybe later. Telling that story may be the death of me," he said grinning. "It'll drain me, and we have work to do."

"How about you tell me at lunch break?"

"Maybe. While I'm sawing, I'll try to remember everything. You're a man now and maybe you can handle it. Hop in the truck and we'll drive down next to the deep gully."

The grandson rode with his grandfather into the steep decline. As they descended into the hollow, his grandfather manhandled the steering wheel dodging the large trees and running over the brush because there was no road through the woods this far in. Pappy was thin, but years working in the forest kept him stout and skilled as a woodsman extraordinaire. Patrick smiled to himself as he recalled the Indiana Jones ride at Disneyland. Don't have to pay for this adventure ride, he smiled within. The log truck leaned to the right and then to the left, and Patrick was lifted off his seat only to crash back down. His grandfather just said, "Hold on tight. We are gonna find out if we need new brakes or not! Have you ever had your face smashed into a windshield?" Unlike Disneyland's Indiana Jones ride, he and his grandfather were not wearing seatbelts in the woods because they had to be ready to jump out of the cab to get things done.

The log truck continued to bounce as it made its way down the steep hill, hitting uneven plots of earth and scraping across the grass and leaves on the forest floor. The double rear tires crushed the small bushes and saplings. They now lay plastered to the forest floor like broken match sticks. Patrick's grandfather maneuvered the log truck and swirled the wheel as he approached the super ravine that divided the steep hills. The truck was now parallel to the ravine, and to Patrick it was like he was now in a different world. It was darker even though there were no clouds in the sky. It was strangely decorated down here deep between the hills. Green moss and ferns covered many of the tree roots and forest floor. There was a coolness down here that the Mississippi summer heat did not zap away. There was no breeze, but the insects flying in and out were peculiarly vivid. Black swallowtail butterflies and the yellow with black borders Tiger swallowtails fluttered in the air and Patrick was about to gaze down into the abyss of the deep ravine when his grandfather called out, "It's pertneer here."

"What's pertneer here?"

"Their secret place."

"It feels like an inner chamber of some kind."

"That's not even the tip of the iceberg. Patrick, if I lay all this out on you right now, I feel like I will be vulnerable."

"To what?"

"To death, it's my heart and soul. No one knows the secret but me now. The Judge never told his son or anyone else. He said that I would understand. It was the Judge who told his son to let me scavenge these trees when they had grown enough to be thinned out. The Judge knew this land and he told me all about it. His son hunted here as a boy, too, but he never desired to learn the Indian ways. I built the wigwam. I spent the nights in these woods, and I listened to the animal sounds at night and heard the voice of an Indian chief calling through the darkness."

"How? Who?"

"That's part of the secret that I still do not know. But these ears have heard a chief calling out in the darkness, and the Judge heard it too. But we never heard it at the same time. Somehow, something knew that he was the Keeper of the Secret and then in these woods a voice or shout like that of an old Chickasaw chief would ring out. The Judge passed everything on to me before he died."

"Did you ever hear it before he told you about the secret?"

"No."

"So how do you know that it was..."

"No, he was. He was a chief because I felt it in my soul. I've only heard that holler three times."

"Would it be Tippahjo?"

"Only if it was his ghost."

"So can you explain the secret now?"

"Son, look around you. You see all these scrubby trees and the ones with their tops broken out from that ice storm three years ago? We have only today to get these out of the bottom here."

"Ok, but at break when we eat our sandwiches, I am ready."

"Are you sure?" Patrick nodded his head for yes. "Maybe by then I will be too."

Patrick's grandfather took the chainsaw and jerked the cord several times. Soon smoke and screeching small engine sounds cut through the tranquility of the moment. Patrick looked at his grandfather and saw a desperate look. His eyes. He did not know if it was about the secret or if he knew with every tree that he cut down, he was taking away a piece of the shade from this land. Up the hill there were pines planted to reforest what had been removed by the settlers who hewed this farmland after the Treaty of Pontotoc in 1832. The virgin forest that had been there when Hernando De Soto had first trampled through North Mississippi was long gone. The early settlers had not cleared all the forests out. The technology and manpower to bring down such huge and massive trees that had taken hundreds of years to grow was not available until long after the Civil War. But when the tree cutters returned, backed by big company money, they did not leave any of the virgin trees. The first trees all came down and that's when the gullies enlarged, and the government finally had to start soil conservation projects decades later. But Patrick knew that his grandfather wanted to leave the land as he knew it. Especially he did not want to touch this sacred-like land wedged between the red dirt hills and the Hatchie Bottom. Little streams flowed from the bottom of the hills, and white sand pools bubbled up with springs that fed into the channels that fed the Hatchie River. Patrick remembered as a lad when his grandfather would bring a hardware pipe when they were hunting and wipe away a few leaves from around the base of the hill near a spring bubbling up. There he would slam the pipe into the hill, pull it out and knock the dirt from the one end and then replace the pipe, and fresh water sprang out of the pipe. He remembered that simple story whenever he heard a preacher preach about Moses striking the rock to get water for the thirsty Israelites. Good tasting cool water came from these hills even in the hot summer. What did he mean by saying that what Ponce De Leon wanted to find was here?

Patrick went over to the edge of the ravine and saw the deep red dirt sides that extended steep from the edges, and he saw where water had made a ditch deep in the center of the ravine. No water flowed now. There was no active stream here. Only when the spring rains come, or the occasional summer thunder bangers did the water flow and make the ravine deeper. Patrick's grandfather was now felling the trees. As the saw's teeth spit out the vivid bark from the base of the tree, smoke collected around the base and then the saw would go silent, and all was quiet until the sound of falling branches popping against the other limbs of nearby trees started. This sound accumulated in intensity until the great big thud pounded the ground as the tree's body slammed into the earth. Patrick stood out of the way as new trees fell until his grandfather started cutting off the branches followed by cutting the trunk into individual pulpwood logs about five and a half feet long. Patrick then bent down and, using his legs, lifted the log and carried it to the log truck bed. Piece by piece the truck framed bed soon had a cover of small stick pulpwood. Patrick no longer felt the cool cathedral-like feeling. Now the mid-morning sun of summer was making its way into the forest especially after the felled trees allowed more sunshine to come in. He was sweating now, and sticky fresh pine rosin was on his leather gloves worn flat with holes in the fingers of one glove. He could smell the fresh pine rosin; its aroma was soothing. Bark specks were on his face and around his wrists underneath his long-sleeved arms. But sawdust was all over his grandfather's face and safety glasses. From foot to head and all clothes in between, anyone would know that his grandfather was running the chainsaw because of the pinewood chips. The mid-morning turned to late morning as Patrick now had almost half the truck bed loaded with pulpwood sticks. They continued to harvest the pines next to the gully. Patrick's grandfather had felled a couple of trees whose tops had hit the gully edge, and he proceeded to cut the tops off. The tops rolled from the ledge all the way into the dry river-like bed in the deepest part of the ravenous red dirt canyon.

Then the unexpected happened. His grandfather cut a tree, and the wind whipped up. As his grandfather tried to push it from its base away from the gully, the wind caught it. The tree was now leaning toward the gully, and its weight sat on the chainsaw. The motor went dead. Immediately all was quiet, and his grandfather yelled, "Patrick! Come quick! Help me push this tree or it's going into the gully!"

Patrick had done this before, and he knew that time was of the essence. He dropped the stick of pulpwood that he had been carrying and ran to the leaning tree. His grandfather was holding the tree back from falling over into the gully. "Grab it up above me and let's push it!"

Patrick grunted and his grandfather grunted as they heaved together. With all the muscle and foot leverage that they could command, the tree would not budge. "Keep holding it while I try to get the saw blade out." Patrick felt the tree leaning more toward him as his grandfather reached for the saw. "Push harder now!" and, as Patrick pushed, his grandfather struggled to remove the chainsaw wiggling it back and forth. The wind slowed and Patrick's heaving barely budged the tree forward just enough to release the trapped saw blade.

"Pappy, we ain't budging it enough to get any momentum in the other direction!"

"Let's try it again." And together they tried with another heave ho. The tree did not go in the opposite direction. "Do you think that you can hold it here while I run to the truck and get the wedge and sledgehammer?"

"That's going to take too long. I'm not sure that I can hold it by myself much longer."

The wind picked up again. Patrick's grandfather hollered, "It's not worth getting you hurt. On the count of three let's both let go and get out of the way." Patrick knew when they let that tree fall that it would pick up speed and the large butt end of the trunk would kick up in the air. But because of the deep gully, as the tree fell into the gully, its butt trunk kicked even higher into the air than Patrick had thought. Where the saw blade had stopped cutting, the little bit of uncut stump ripped free and the butt end of the tree almost popped Patrick in his lower jaw. He could feel the whoosh of air as his reflexes moved his body out of the way just in the nick of time. "Whew! That was too close."

"I hate to lose that tree. I would not have cut one that large, but its top was damaged back in the ice storm." They watched the long tree as it lay all the way into the deepest part of the ravine, its butt trunk stood about three feet in the air. "I might be able to cut that butt trunk for a piece of pulpwood if you think you can handle holding it and keeping it from rolling down in the ravine. If it starts rolling, there's not much'n you can do about it."

Patrick was contemplating if he should attempt to hold that much weight of a log when out of nowhere, he felt the first razor-like sharp sting on his neck. Then his elbow. Then under the cuff of his holey glove. His grandfather yelled one word, "Yellowjackets!" The fallen tree had landed with a broken sharp limb stabbing directly into a yellowjacket nest nestled high in the red dirt steeped slope on the side of the gully. Before their brains could think, the legs of both men started running up the inclined hill. They passed the log truck. Both ran so fast that their working gloves slung off into the air. They jumped briars and pine branches and instinctively raised their booted feet high when in honeysuckle vines. Thick long briars ripped through their jeans. Patrick didn't feel the pain of the briars because as he was running, he was slapping himself on his arms and neck where he felt the stinging. He had a long-sleeve work shirt, but the stings were coming through the shirt. Then he felt a sting on his calf. He hopped and ran as he slapped to stop the stinging by killing the aggressive yellowjackets. Then it got worse. He felt something crawling up his britches leg past his knee. As he slapped his pants, they were so thick that the pants actually protected the avenger pests beneath. Then for the first time, he felt the buzzing past his knee inside his pants and it was headed north. He was still hoping and running but grabbed his leg about the pocket area as the buzzing was going for his crotch area. Finally, Patrick stuck his hand in his pants pocket. There he could grab the devilish insect through the soft cloth pocket, and it stung his finger as he grabbed it, but he kept it from getting farther north in his britches.

Out of breath and finally away from the offending yellow jackets, he noticed that his grandfather in his 70s had outrun him to the top of the hill. "How many stings did you get?"

"At least ten or twelve."

"I think I got three. A fourth varmint was about to sting me, but I hit him so hard I think that I knocked his stinger off. Boy, I'm gonna have a bruise there tomorrow on my left arm. Let's rest awhile. Let them settle down, and I will walk back down there and get the water and our lunch. Just blow a minute under the shade here. I didn't get stung as bad as you did. I got some chewing tobacco back in the truck. I'll chew some up and make some tobacco juice to put on those stings."

"You got anything else in the truck? Like a first aid kit?"

"Yep, but it just has Band-Aids and some dried-up ointment.

"Bring the dried-up ointment back with you. You can have the tobacco juice for yours, and I'll spit on that dried up ointment to put on my stings."

"Suit yourself, but that backy will draw that poison out of the wounds. I promise you."

"I'll still try the ointment first. At least it'll be my spit."

"If you would have taken up the tobacco habit, you could chew your own."

"Well, if you had not given me that first chew when I was just 6 years old, I might be chewing it today."

His grandfather laughed and said, "Your mother's still mad at me for that. But you know, I probably did your health some good because you have never chewed since and you have never even smoked have you?"

"No, sir."

"Just rest, I'll go and fetch the water jug."

Chapter 2

Patrick sat on the top of the ridge hill. Hidden in the clump of trees was the topography of the land. Patrick looked up to the little rise that was subtle but crested a couple of hundred feet from where he was sitting. There he always remembered the designation that his grandfather had taught him from an early age. From that crest you could stand and spit. If you spat toward the sunrise or the east, then when it rained it would carry your spittle north into the Hatchie River, which flowed north into the Mississippi River. But if you spat toward the sunset or the west then the spittle would flow with the rainwater toward the south into the Tallahatchie River which also emptied into the Mississippi River. His grandfather had an old record player that would spin with an old 45 small, pressed record Patrick would play over and over as a child. The title song he was told was a top hit back in the 1960s. It was titled "Ode to Billie Joe." And the haunting lyrics now swirled in Patrick's head as the hurts of the stings left him a bit nauseated. His head throbbed and heat swirled about him to the point he wondered if he might just faint. He could feel his stings swelling, but he closed his eyes and mentally he could see that old 45 spinning on the record player and hear that needle hitting some scratches in the record but spewing forth the chorus, "And Billie Joe McAllister jumped off the Tallahatchie Bridge."

Suicide and death had never really registered in Patrick's mind, but he listened as the lyrics swirled round and round and the verses ran together about sitting at the supper table and passing the peas and the preacher coming to dinner and saying that Billie Joe McAllister had last been seen by this girl at the table. The haunting death and the flowers and the cousin who ran a store in Tupelo and how the entire song just haunted him with its lyrics. Now he was still hot and breathing hard and sweating like a fever rising because of the yellowjackets' stings.

His grandfather broke the spell with the words, "Drink you some of the water from the jug. That will make you feel better."

Patrick grabbed the thermos jug, opened the lid and swigged down the cool drink. He did feel better. He was still too hot to eat his sandwich, and the nausea from the stings left him not hungry for now. His grandfather sat on the ground beside him. They both leaned back on the large post oak tree which gave them shade from the sun. He reached over to take the jug from Patrick's hand and took a drink. "When I was just a boy, this tree was in the middle of a cotton field that was all over this ridge. I picked cotton here, and I rested under this tree and had a jug of water to drink from. In fact, because I was so young, they would send me down on the other side of this ridge to the springs there. The purtiest white sand in a little bubbling pool of water that was always clean and cool, and no matter how dry a summer ever got, they say that this spring has never stopped flowing." The grandfather paused, then said, "Yes, I think the time has come to let you know what I know."

"About the secret!"

"Yessum."

"You've taught me so much," Patrick's voice was giddy with excitement. "Teachers in school have always wondered where I got so much information about the Native Americans and their history. We've walked so much of this land from hunting to hiking and coming through it during the winter snows, and that time the ice storm came, all the trees were bending over like angels bowing down in the brilliant sunlight like we were in a crystal palace. I will never forget all those times and seeing these woods in so many different seasons. I think that my favorite season is still the fall when the trees turn with their leaves of many colors and the animals store up for winter and the cool refreshing air feels so wonderful after a hot summer like this one. Boy, I would like to have some of that fall air right now blowing on my face like a fan."

"Yep. If I were a leaf, I would feel like it's fall. I feel like my sap is starting to drop and my leaf is turning golden."

"But you outran me up this hill when the yellowjackets started stinging us."

"Well, you know Caleb took the hill in Hebron when the Israelites crossed the Jordan River. And he was eighty years old, and he was fighting against giants. Something about this land right here energizes me. Somehow whatever got into Caleb, I think I get some of what he had when I'm here in these hills."

Patrick smiled and smirked a laugh and said, "There's no giants to fight against around here."

"There was a battle not far from here though. And it was like giants being fought."

"I didn't know there was a Civil War battle around here. I've searched for Minie balls from battle sites all around North Mississippi, but you never told me that there was a battle on these lands. I've never heard anyone say there were even any major troop movements on the Judge's land during the war."

"I didn't say the Civil War. And long before the famous Chickasaw battle of Ackia down around Tupelo that kept us from speaking French even today."

"What battle then?"

"That's part of the secret."

"But now I have to know."

"It's time. But my mouth's dry. Let me go fetch some more water first. This jug is empty."

"You going to go down like Moses to the spring?"

"Yep."

"Watch out for those water moccasins."

"Yep, reckon I will. That spring water will be good for ya."

"Yep, I reckon it will. Thanks, Pappy."

Patrick sat under the shade and felt a relinquishing breeze. He smiled thinking about the "Ode to Billy Joe McAllister" and he thought about Elvis. The home at his Tupelo birthplace was so small. He remembered his grandfather telling him about being there in Tupelo when Elvis came back home to sing at the big fair there. How in the 1950s Elvis became the King of Rock 'n Roll. And he thought of one of his favorites, "I'm All Shook-up." With the yellowjacket stings still throbbing, he felt more than just shook up maybe a little delirious. It's like the music on this piece of earth was like a boxing ring where, instead of boxers, it was the people who made the music, battling it out on this land that William Faulkner called his little postage stamp of earth. In his disoriented state Patrick could see his favorite singers battling with their songs on his postage stamp shaped like a boxing ring as the world watched and danced and sang along. Artist after artist he could see in that boxing-like ring pouring out their hearts and souls with guitars, drums, saxophones, keyboards—why he could see the Killer, Jerry Lee Lewis, with smoke coming from his fingers as he stroked piano keys on fire. Singers bellowed into microphones—B.B. King, Muddy Waters, Mick Jagger, Lennon and McCartney, Bono, Whitney Houston, Tina Turner and on and on and on in a glorious vision of sound, sight, and soul within a wheeling circle of song and dance...

"Got the coolest, freshest, best tasting water on earth right here as if it was from the Garden of Eden," his grandfather broke the Samuel Coleridge-like visual hallucinational state. "Now where do I start with the story? Well, first let me fill you in on some family history that ties us to the Judge's family. You know that I told you a long time ago that my great-great-grandmother was Chickasaw."

"Yeah. I'm always proud of that."

"There have been times when white folks in Mississippi tried to hide their native heritage---and their black heritage, too! But let me tell you this. You see, when the Treaty of Pontotoc was signed back in the 1830s, one of the local chiefs had twin teenage daughters. One fell in love with a white settler named Simpson, and the other fell in love with a man named Turnball. Neither daughter wanted to move to Oklahoma. The chief did not like the treaty, but he was chief of a small village and did not really have any power in the treaty talks. He really did not like the white settlers that wanted to marry his daughters, but he gave in when he realized that his daughters would not be forced off the Chickasaw lands because they were married to the settlers. Now the way that they met the settlers was from the missionary who came to preach to the tribes. In one village not but about twenty miles from here near the Tippah County and Union County line today, there was this great Christian revival. It happened during what some people now call the Second Great Awakening. I don't know the missionary's name, but he came and stirred up the area with his preaching so that the squatters and frontiersmen and all the Indians in the village came night after night. Now with the movies and all, when you think about the wild West, you think west of the Mississippi River; but back in those days the wild West was basically the state of Mississippi and maybe western Tennessee. Now at this point there had not been a treaty signed, so that only white squatters were trickling in and there were no slaves in the land except what the Chickasaw had back then because the government could take away any property of squatters. They said that there was a singing and a preaching; and with nothing else back in those days to do, everybody within 25 miles would saddle up their horses or walk to come to the revival. Squatters would load up their families in wagons to make the journey for spiritual enhancement or entertainment, but they all came. The preacher had been to one of the great revivals that happened in Cane Ridge, Kentucky, and he brought that excitement down to the Chickasaws. Now they had seen missionaries and had heard them. A few of the Indians became converted, but with this revival almost everybody it seems was converted as they fell into the spirit in trance-like states and, thus, all the talk about that Chickasaw revival even years later. But that is where Mr. Simpson and Mr. Turnball met their future wives. Mr. Simpson was the Judge's great-grandfather, Mr. Turnball was killed in the Civil War, and his Chickasaw wife remarried my great-great-grandfather. I think that is one of the reasons that the Judge always took a liking to me and taught me all about the Chickasaws and then passed on the secret that he had learned from Tippahjo.

"So, are you ready to tell me about the secret?"

"Yes! I'm getting there. First let me show you a piece, of the secret."

"A piece?"

"Let's get up and move over to the two dirt tracks, made by the truck riding on this ridge-top, dirt road. Just sit there in the dirt."

Patrick moved to the dirt and had a seat. His grandfather reached down and started scooping up fine dust of sandy dirt. He let it flow from his fist like salt flowing out of an open container. In silence he continued to scoop and release, scoop and release.

"What are you doing?"

"Sssshhh, just listen."

Patrick didn't hear anything but the buzzing of the flies that had found them. As his grandfather continued to scoop and release the sandy dirt, Patrick started to hear the wind in the trees, birds chirping; a hawk directly overhead flapping its wings.

"Patrick, you know that verse that so many people talk about in the Book of Chronicles?"

"The one about praying and God healing this land?"

"Yep, that one. Well, being Keeper of the Secret brings new meaning to that verse. Take your boots off, and your socks off."

They both removed their boots and socks and were sitting on the dirt pathway. The grandfather stood up and grabbed the water jug full of the fresh spring water. He poured water into the parched dry sandy dirt. He reached down and scooped up the mud.

"God has healed this land and with this land you shall be healed." Patrick's grandfather proceeded to wipe the mud over Patrick's neck and face where he had been stung. Without saying anything Patrick rolled back his long shirt sleeves to expose the stings for the application of the healing mud. And then he pulled up his pants legs for the same. Then his grandfather took some dry dirt and let it flow over Patrick's head. Then he took the water jug and poured water over Patrick's head until the dirt and mud were washed away. "I need to remember more parts from the Bible."

"So, what parts in the Bible, Pappy?

"Somewhere in Kings and Chronicles. Don't ask me first or second because I can't remember. But when it talks about Solomon's ships sailing to far ports. Don't laugh now, but Tippahjo said that he knew for a fact that those ships of King Solomon came up the Mississippi River. Where did the name Mississippi come from and why is it important? First, did you know that the word millionaire came from the word Mississippi? It did. Goes back to the Mississippi Bubble. All these things were happening in France, and people wanted these bonds called Mississippi bonds because these bonds involved the lands of the Louisiana Purchase well before that happened. The Mississippi bonds were in so much demand and people were making so much money that Mississippi bond holders began to be called millionaires. Sounds kind of crazy, doesn't it?"

"Sure, if you looked at Mississippi today, you wouldn't think about the word millionaire."

"Well, who knows? Maybe the word millionaire and Mississippi will be tied together again someday. But that part of the word Mississippi was after Hernando DeSoto discovered the river. Before the Chickasaws ever came to these lands, there was another indigenous people who lived here. The Chickasaws and the Choctaws and maybe the Cherokee and other nations could be and probably are descendants from these first peoples. They built the big Indian mounds around the South that we see today, just like the one near Natchez and others on the Natchez Trace. These Indians were the first Native Americans, but, of course, there was no America back then. The civilizations existing then were contacted by King Solomon's ships from the ancient country of Israel." Patrick's grandfather stared at him in his eyes and said, "I'm not kidding now. Tippahjo said that they sailed right up the Mississippi River, and somewhere around the high bluffs of modern-day Memphis, they entered this land. There was a meeting, and these ships came back and forth more than twice, but we don't know how many times. But on the second visit they brought something extra special. Now Patrick, don't sit there with your bottom jaw dropped so wide. Do you want to hear this story or not?"

"Yes, sir. Is this in the Bible?"

"Not exactly but, yes, it says King Solomon's ships sailed to far off lands. And I think that those lands include here."

"With these yellowjacket stings and this heat, I was beginning to think that you were maybe just someone talking in a dream. You just told me that King Solomon's ships, the King Solomon from the

Bible, the son of King David who killed the giant, Goliath, we are talking about this same King Solomon, aren't we?"

"Yelp." His grandfather puckered his lips on the p in yelp to give it a popping sound emphasizing an end to that thought of Patrick's words. "Now as I tell you this, I am going to get you to say three times what I had to say. I am the Keeper of the Secret, and I will tell no other about these words of which I am about to hear."

Patrick's grandfather had him repeat the words three times in succession, and then he added, "But when I know through my spirit flowing with this land and with its hills and creeks and wildlife true, that when that day comes to pass on this secret, then to him or her alone shall I pass this secret to." Patrick saw a firm and unusual gaze that he had never seen in his grandfather's eyes. "Will you do this, my son?"

"Yes, I will."

"Somewhere in these hills, not far from where we stand, there is something buried. No one ever saw it for hundreds of years; I guess for over 2500 years for sure. Until once. But before I tell you about that one time, let me tell you what is part of the treasure. This is the only part of the secret that has been passed down, sacred and simple, as there is thought to be more than just what I am about to tell you."

Patrick now sat as if he was in another world. He was oblivious to the heat and the stings and the day's work to be finished. He thought about his English literature teacher when she read about Samuel Taylor Coleridge and the Ancient Mariner, and now his grandfather took on that role as if he was talking about ghosts and "Water, water everywhere and nor a drop to drink" or something even more unimaginable just a few short minutes ago.

"You see, King Solomon cemented a treaty by delivering two gold chalices, cups of some sort that were designed and perfected into being by the craftsmen of the Temple there in Jerusalem. In that time the Temple was a wonder of all the world, and the goldsmiths there were the best ever. And from there seven gold cups were fabricated with divine inspiration for the then seven kingdoms of the known world. Two of these cups were sent up the Mississippi River, one for the kingdom east of the Mississippi and one cup for the one west of the Mississippi. These gold chalices were to be held in a secret location until the ships came back and announced a planned day of all the kingdoms of the world to meet in Jerusalem with King Solomon. Tippahjo did not say who the other kingdoms were. I would guess, but I do not know this for sure, that it was probably Israel, Egypt, China, Europe and South America. I do not know, but this I do know that one of the gold cups was not only seen but taken some time after Hernando DeSoto came through. He was following leads and rumors about this stash of gold. All the secret that was ever passed on was about the two gold chalices. But if King Solomon's ships delivered the chalices there had to be more gold because the Bible says that King Solomon had more gold than anyone else in the world. DeSoto was on to something.

Before he discovered the Mississippi River, he traveled through North Mississippi and historians don't know exactly where his trek was. But I know."

"What?"

"The battle that I told you about was his battle. It wasn't a major battle in history books, but it was a major battle for DeSoto and his soldiers. You see, DeSoto was near here. Right here about here Tippahjo said. That's why you cannot talk about the secret, and the battle is part of the secret. I wanted long ago to tell you about this area when you would take that metal detector of yours and go out to Civil War battlefields and look for Minie balls and belt buckles and such. Don't know if you would ever find anything from the 1540s around here, but this is where a Chickasaw outpost was. I say an outpost because the Chickasaw were charged with keeping the secret, and most, except Chiefs and the Keeper of the Secret, never knew of the secret, or if they got wind of it, they never knew where it was located. The Natchez Trace doesn't run today where it once ran. It was only about a mile from these hills, and there were several Indian paths and trails that ran through these hills, but the Natchez Trace was a major Indian transportation route, and the Chickasaw kept the equivalent of a command post not far from these hills. Now the Chickasaw were tribal and traveled with the seasons without a permanent camp. But because of the Natchez Trace, they kept a command post to sort of guard the trail but, really they were guarding the secret! Now some of the warriors would keep their families there from time to time but this post was permanent so there were cave-like structures built into the hills for the permanent post. Tippahjo said that the Chickasaw villages all over the area had a system so that the outpost was always fortified. The Keeper of the Secret was always nearby, and all the Chickasaws thought it was to guard the Trace, but in reality he was there to guard the secret!"

"Wow an Indian garrison was near here!"

"You have seen it. Locals know about it. It's not on the Judge's land; it's about a mile over on the Tombigbee Ridge. The Chickasaws knew better than to have the garrison at the secret hiding place. And as Hernando DeSoto zeroed in from rumors and possibly torture of some Indians, no one knows how he came to this area, but he made his first winter camp right on the Tombigbee Ridge. And I have shown you the cave-like structures, but I never told you what they were. To this day most Indian historians don't even know about them. But they would be baffled because it does not fit the narrative of Chickasaws moving their villages seasonally. But they don't know about the secret, and I could not talk about it, but, oh, how I wish that I could! But some kind of curse-like spiritual mechanism keeps me from breaking my oath. I know that with the ties to King Solomon there is something that may even be connected to the planets and stars spiritually speaking, but it's more than a small country church deacon can fully understand. I just have never figured it out. But when the Bible speaks of principalities of the air, and you hang out in these Hatchie Bottom lands sometimes the hair stands on the edge of your skin. It can get downright spooky just as if someone or something is watching your every move. You've been down here in the night and heard the bobcats and the howling coyotes. I swear they say there are no panthers east of the Mississippi, but I know that I have heard a sound deep in these woods that sounds just like a big cat–not some little bobcat! And they were here when the settlers started coming in to settle this land. The Chickasaws told stories about the panthers in these woods from long back further than anyone alive today could ever know."

"I've never heard you talk about panthers down here in these woods."

"I've never seen any, but that doesn't mean they don't exist. I'm sure that the Hatchie Bottom has yet to reveal all that revels deep beneath its quagmire domes."

"Now what about these two gold cups?"

"Mantachie, a legendary medicine man, knew about and saw at least one golden chalice from the secret hiding place. Mantachie took one chalice into battle down near Tupelo in the Battle of Ackia in 1736. And that was a real battle. It was like a mini-world war back then that saw nations aligned in both the Indian world and the white man's world, and, in fact, the black man's world was involved, too. Red, white, and black! It gave the French the real blues because they never recovered from their loss at Ackia. You can argue that the Battle of Ackia set the continent up for the French and Indian War that a young George Washington set off. So never forget the significance of Ackia. And somehow in that battle the Chickasaws thoroughly won, but the golden chalice was lost as far as Tippahjo knew. Mantachie's son was just sworn in as a Keeper of the Secret because Mantachie was like a standard bearer and a general surgeon to Chief Tanglefoot. Mantachie went to be by Chief Tanglefoot's side during the battle, but neither he nor the chief nor the golden chalice ever returned to these lands. But only one of the two golden chalices was taken by Mantachie and all the Keepers of the Secret since then have assumed the other one is still in the secret spot."

"Which is where, now?"

"That's the part of the secret that was never passed down except that it is on the Judge's land somewhere. Tippahjo said that for sure."

"Do you know about where?"

"I can remember vaguely as a child when most of these pine trees were young. The open fields were being planted in pine. Back then just like about every field acre in Mississippi, there was nothing but cotton planted just about everywhere. In the fall you would see white lint along the highways that made it look like it had just snowed. The schools would let out during cotton picking season, and all the kids would be picking cotton for either their parents or for neighbors. Just as I was a child, the mechanical cotton pickers started to slowly change that. But I remember seeing this ridge on which we stand and that deep ravine and the ridge on the opposite side. Well, there is a swell of land. Look as the trees rise and then continue to rise and slope with curves and then again to the sky. Now you see trees, but you can still see the curves of the treetops sloping up and down. When this was farmland for crops, you could have seen it best. And before the deep ravine ravished through the land, it would have been even more like a body lying down."

"I'm not really following what you are saying right now."

"I know I'm not making a lot of sense. But look to the rises. Come, let's move out into the clearing a little and where you can better see the flow of the land. I distinctly remember, before I ever knew about the secret, seeing the flow like a pregnant lady lying down on the earth. That swell of land like a baby inside her womb and the washed-out ravine is preparing for a time of labor and birth. I believe that somewhere near the ravine and into that swell of land is where the secret is stored. I often thought after I became the Keeper of the Secret that there must be a cave or entrance for the gold chalice to have been removed but I have never found one."

"Have you ever brought out a metal detector?"

"No, I just feel like as Keeper of the Secret it is mine to keep and not to seek. If the land is intertwined and the history is weaved into what we know today and the ancient Israelites and the original Solomon's built Temple's gold chalices, then who am I to dig into this land and what in the world would I do if I were to find the secret? It's not like I can tell the world."

"Shittim bark."

"No need to bring up that forest in Israel."

"If I now know the secret and I can't tell it either then how do I quelch this desire to start looking?"

"First, there is a curse. There is always only one Keeper of the Secret, and only the Keeper of the Secret or a chief can touch the gold chalice that is hidden. If anyone else touches it, there is a curse that a dark day will come. Violence will be unleashed on this land and the land itself will become violent! Only when the other chalice bearers show another gold chalice can the Keeper of the Secret retrieve the hidden gold cup. You are now a part of something bigger than you and me. Bigger than the Chickasaw Nation and bigger than the United States and bigger than this physical world that we now know. Just to know the secret is bearing a burden few have ever known. The reason that we bear this secret is not for personal gain; in fact, it will keep you humble and tied to this land. But you are now a part of something that you watch and guard and most importantly---you wait. You know that verse in the Bible about waiting upon the Lord? Well, as Keeper of the Secret we wait. When the time is proper, the secret will unfold to you and you will know what to do. That's what I've been told, and I believe that. Now you must believe that, too. If, and when, another gold chalice comes before you then, somehow, someway you will know how to find what is hidden."

"Starship to earth! Am I on a new planet? So just why did King Solomon send ships up the Mississippi River?"

"Oh, Tippahjo said that the first Americans, or should I say the first people group, because they were here before the Chickasaw and long before it was called the Americas, civilizations were diverse evidently because King Solomon's ship captain designated an East and a West king or chief. Supposedly he was fascinated by the huge river and thought that each side deserved its own golden chalice. How he did this I don't know, but the seven gold chalices were for the Seven Kingdoms of all the earth that were to come together in Jerusalem for a special feast designed and planned by King Solomon. This feast was to be held about ten years from when the gold cups were delivered. It was to be a peace feast unlike any other ever. Because of the different arrival times, the feast and festivities were to last six full months. For whatever reasons we don't know, it never happened. Maybe the ship's captain and crew went down in a storm or communications were severed somehow forever. But you know that the tales of the first explorers to the New World are full of the first people groups saying that a far-off fair-skinned people would return."

Patrick's grandfather paused to glance deeper into Patrick's eyes, and then continued, "King Solomon was the wisest man ever to walk upon the earth says the Bible, of course, that was before the New Testament. The Bible tells us that because it says King Solomon was given understanding more so than any man ever before. So, he built the first temple in Jerusalem and grand buildings, but he built something even better during his reign. He built world peace—the world was at peace for 40 years as he reigned on the throne in Israel. He came in peace up the Mississippi River unlike Hernando DeSoto whose careless disregard for the natives and search for gold was wrapped around his desire for power and conquest. He especially treated the Chickasaw with contempt. Now when Hernando DeSoto set winter camp in 1542, he was near the secret–he just didn't know it. DeSoto and his men in his expedition called the area Quizquiz.

Like I said, he was just a mile away as the crow flies. The Keeper of the Secret knew how close the Spaniards were. The garrison there was very important. Hernando DeSoto as a military man, I think he knew there was a reason that this garrison was not a typical Indian village. He knew that this certain village, even with its wigwams, still had permanent structures. Many of DeSoto's men were ready to leave. There is an old book written by a soldier who went with Hernando DeSoto on his expeditions, and he wrote a diary of his trips. And I remember reading about their time and their winter camp in North Mississippi. It was not a good memory for the Spaniards. The soldier stated that the bad relations with the Chickasaws started long before their winter camp. All along Desoto's journey, he found interpreters, and some Indian interpreters were Chickasaw, but others were Natchez, Cherokee, Choctaw, and other tribes. The soldier told how one of the Spaniard's African slaves escaped to live with the native 'heathen' locals. The soldier writing the story of the expedition could not understand how a human, even though a slave, would want to live not with the Christian Spaniards but with the heathen unbelieving Indians. He wrote that the Spaniards all would have frozen to death during an exceptionally cold winter except for a natural plant of the region. Supposedly they cut this native plant and weaved it into blankets for protection and warmth. Which plant that was I don't rightly know, but I've always suspected that it was the sage grass that grows openly in these fields around here. And of course, the Spaniards brought with them a couple of vices for which the Chickasaw were not prepared to resist temptation. The soldier talked about how the Chickasaw could not refuse any 'fire water' or alcoholic beverage coming from the stores of the Spaniards. And the second vice which they had never encountered was any part of a pig. The Chickasaw, once they tasted bacon or ham or any part of the pig, it became a delicacy for which they would steal to taste again. In fact, relations between the Indian tribes and the Spaniards went to an international low when Hernando DeSoto used a heavy hand with his onsite Spanish court to find two Indians guilty of stealing a pig. Of course, DeSoto knew that it was very important to have living animals for food on an expedition. That's why they traveled with live animals; even though the creatures slowed down the movement of the journey. As the old timers would say, you can eat everything the pig offers except the squeal. But when DeSoto decided execution by hanging was the punishment for stealing the pig, the Chickasaw Nation went crazy—and rightly so. After the executions of the two Chickasaw warriors were carried out everything went downhill. If DeSoto thought that he would be able to find gold and to discover its secret hiding place by bribing or sweet talking their chief, he never had a chance after he executed the two Chickasaw warriors. In fact, because of the Keeper of the Secret, the chief mobilized his warriors, and every night they would surround the Spanish winter camp. The Native Americans would holler and yell and vocalize all kinds of animal shrieks and cries. Of course, all these sounds unnerved the Spaniards. It was winter, but many of the Spaniards were still spooked by the native fireflies or lightning bugs that they had seen for the first time in their lives during the summer. Some thought of these as evil spirits spying on them. After about two weeks of terrifying rituals, the Chickasaws attacked at night with bows and arrows. And some arrows they lit with fire. The battle caught the Spaniards off guard, and by the time the Spaniards retrieved and loaded their muskets, the Chickasaws had faded back from the battle. But the Spaniards did get some shots off with their muskets. The Chickasaws lost a few Warriors for the first time by bullet or 'firesticks.' The Chickasaw Warriors who were shot did not know what the round holes in their bodies were. Some wandered in the woods in pain for hours and were found dead the following day. Unaware of what magic dark spell had caused the opening into their body and how it led to death, the Keeper of the Secret pondered with the Chickasaw chief if the Spaniards were coming to claim the golden chalices for the meeting in that far off land called Jerusalem. The chief sent the Keeper of the Secret to a face-to-face meeting with Hernando DeSoto. The Keeper of the Secret inquired of Hernando DeSoto through interpreters about the land called Jerusalem. DeSoto, knowing nothing of the secret gold chalices, only said that Jerusalem had been taken over by the followers of Muhammad. Because DeSoto did not know anything more about Jerusalem and a feast of kings, the secret hiding place would remain secret. The Keeper of the Secret had thought that if these Spaniards had a golden chalice, then they would have mentioned it to him. He gave DeSoto a chance, but DeSoto obviously knew nothing of a grand feast. The Keeper of the Secret already sensed that the darkness surrounding the Spaniards was not related to the ancient stories of the ships from King Solomon that had sailed in peace with special valuable gifts up the Mississippi River ages ago. The Keeper of the Secret told DeSoto that he and his men should continue their journey. He wanted the Spaniards far away from the secret hiding place and wanted them to go. That night the chief sent his warriors once again to verbally harass the Spaniards. The next day DeSoto made the decision to leave this winter camp. The Spaniards went west, toward the great river that they had been told about. The Keeper of the Secret had kept the Spanish away, and that was the first time that Europeans came close to the secret chamber."

"How did you know all of that? Did Tippahjo tell all that to the Judge?"

"Nope, Tippahjo talked only about the fighting against DeSoto and wondering at the first if there was a connection between the Spaniards and the ship sent long ago by King Solomon. But the Keeper of the Secret said that this land itself rejected Hernando DeSoto. He said that the sky and the land conversed with the waters to urge DeSoto to get away. But you didn't catch an important detail in that story, did you son?"

"What detail is that?"

"Well, the Indians or first people's group were fascinated by King Solomon's ships."

"What do you mean? Were they huge or what?"

"These people had never seen a ship that could sail upstream, but King Solomon's ships did."

"So, King Solomon used something that was never possible before the steam engine? Wow, what did those ships use?"

"It's been lost to history and no clue to what his ships used to do so, but it must have fascinated all the first people who saw that; the Chickasaw knew that if the Spaniards couldn't sail up the "Father of Waters," then they probably didn't have the golden chalice. Now remember that as I tell you the rest of the story. You see, DeSoto was not a man of his word. When DeSoto had the two Chickasaws executed, he thought that he was putting down a strict rule of law to stop the Indians from thievery, but the Indians did not clue into the European's sense of justice which was completely unjustified. The Keeper of the Secret then consulted with the chief and together they decided that DeSoto himself must pay a high price for the execution order. As you know, the Spaniards record that DeSoto was sickened after he discovered the Mississippi River and then was secretly buried in the river after he died. The Spaniards did not want the Indians to have access to his corpse so that is why they buried him in the Mississippi River. What they don't tell us in history is that the chief secretly had been poisoning DeSoto all along his way toward the Mississippi River. The Keeper of the Secret made sure that different villages along the way, as DeSoto and his men moved toward the Mississippi River, kept giving only DeSoto food and special meals that slowly poisoned him so that he paid the price that was determined by the chief of the garrison village. DeSoto thought he was being singled out as the leader for special meals; but, in fact, he was weakening his body so much that not long after he saw the great Mississippi River, the river itself became his coffin so to speak. Again, the Spanish did not want the Indians to discover his grave and misuse his corpse—because they knew the Chickasaws were still furious about his execution of the two warriors who had only stolen a pig."

"Man, where were these stories in my history classes? I've never heard such stories and I've lived here all my life!"

"Well, you are like me now. You know the truth, but I am the Keeper of the Secret, and you will become the Keeper of the Secret when I can no longer do the job. We cannot tell the whole world this story because it's all part of the secret---the secret that is bound to this land and locked into the ongoing plan from the ships of King Solomon to the many chiefs who have engaged with the secret, hoping that one day all their efforts will see success. A day when the secret buried in these hills will come to fruition and this land will fulfill its purpose of peace and prosperity blossoming like a flower releasing its petals with a fresh aroma of peace for all for generations."

"Ongoing? Do you really believe that the golden chalices buried here..."

"Golden chalice, remember that one is missing."

"Well, then the golden chalice. Do you ever wonder that for all these years, that maybe whatever is hidden in these hills will all have been for nothing?"

"Not once. We have Chickasaw blood running through our veins. To think that we have been honored to have been asked to fulfill what is an ongoing legacy for not hundreds but maybe 3,000 years. Now how many people who have ever lived on this earth can say that they were a part of something so honoring? And nobody, and I mean nobody, has an incklin' or a clue to what me and you now know. It is indeed an honor that will not be on my tombstone but etched in the eternal sky forever like the stars tell their stories, and so will I and now so will you. Believe me, you will live your story well. They will know---the stars will know. I do not know how but this I do know. We have been called forward, elected so to speak. It's as if angels are watching us. It's as if the very stars above us are guiding us and watching over this land, too. In these woods whether at night or in the day, I can always feel like Chickasaw eyes from the past are watching me. Enough so that the hair on my arms will rise, not in fear, but just as if there is a presence in these woods watching, comforting, and proud that the Keeper of the Secret is still standing guard."

"Do I get to carry something special?"

"You mean like a spear or a staff or something?"

"Well, maybe not a spear but I thought that there may be a passing of something, like a knife or a hatchet or a necklace or something."

His grandfather reached beneath his neck under his shirt.

"There is something."

"What's that? A tiny arrowhead?"

"Look closely. It's a special one. It's an arrowhead shaped by the Chickasaws from a fossilized saber tooth tiger's canine tooth. When I pass away, it is yours."

"Wow! That is awesome—so cool!" His grandfather winked and placed the necklace arrowhead back. Patrick continued, "And you think that the secret hiding place may very well be around right here where we are working today?"

"I told you to look at the lay of the land. It's like a woman about to give birth."

"Yeah. I can see that. It looks like she is about to push a newborn baby out right down there into the ravine right now even."

"Well, she ain't gone into contractions of childbirth. At least not now."

"And what good does knowing the secret do if we can't tell anyone?"

"You must use the Chickasaw in you. Tune in. Listen to your Chickasaw blood. It's like this land has chosen you just like it chose me and the Judge and would not let Tippahjo ever leave even when President Andrew Jackson and all the forces of the federal government told him he had to go. It's the land, Patrick. You are a part of the secret and bound to this land-every hill and creek and round mound of dirt and every field and stream and dry rain bed gully knows that you, Patrick, you are to be the new Keeper of the Secret! And this land and earth, this dirt and rock and sky and waters all around here now know that! They know you! It chooses us and when it does, we will be here to make sure no one or nothing starts digging or exploring or cuts up with just pure mischief. I patrol the land to keep its secret."

Chapter 3

Patrick no longer felt the sting of the yellowjackets. The healing water and sand mud worked. As Pappy told of the secret, Patrick had rested, and had eaten his lunch, and now in early afternoon wanted to know more. Both Pappy and Patrick sat beneath the large oak. Patrick continued his conversation, "But what about the missing gold cup? And you said that was the first battle with the Europeans."

"That's right. It was the first battle with the Europeans, the Spaniards. The next major battle (and I mean it was major) well that one happened with the French. That was a couple of hundred years later, and as I have told you before, it is the very reason that we don't speak French here today. You can remember by thinking in centennial segments. DeSoto in the 1540s, the French around 1740, Andrew Jackson and the Trail of Tears around the 1840s and the 1940s are getting near about into my childhood. Now, Tippahjo said that as the Keeper of the Secret and the chiefs got together, they decided to move the village away from the garrison and only have warriors at the garrison for a rotation from different villages so that it was not a major stopping place on the Natchez Trace. You got to remember that the Native Americans used the Natchez Trace like a major highway would be used today for their civilization. From today's Natchez, Mississippi, all the way to Nashville, Tennessee, the Natchez Trace was the main road used for hundreds of years for all the different tribes. Then when the white man came, it became a wagon trail vastly utilized until the steam engine made it possible for settlers to go upstream on the rivers. Over the two hundred years since Hernando DeSoto came through the Chickasaws slowly rerouted the Natchez Trace to go through, near what is Tupelo today where the Battle of Ackia was fought. And then the French wanted to declare all this land east of the Mississippi for France, too. (They already had most of the land west of the Mississippi like what would later be the Louisiana Purchase.) And in what could be called a mini-world war, the French and the Chickasaw fought it out in what the history books call the Battle of Ackia. Because the Natchez Trace had been rerouted, the Chickasaw garrison or fort that was there was moved away from the buried secret. When the French came to Ackia, they did not know that the British trappers and frontiersmen had taught the Chickasaw how to build a fort out of timber and how to shoot muskets. The French thought that the Chickasaw would be just like the same Chickasaw warriors that Hernando DeSoto had fought. In fact, just as the British had allied with the Chickasaw, the French brought with them a free black African general and his black African slave fighters and the French also had German mercenaries like those who fought at Trenton in the Revolutionary War. And some of the Choctaw warriors sided with the French, and some Cherokee came to help the Chickasaw as a few Indian warriors sided independently with both sides. So, you see, it was really a precursor of a world war. Now because the French did not have good communication, the battle plan was not carried out very well. The French were going to surprise attack from two directions with two different armies. One French army was to invade by coming up the Mobile River from the Mobile Bay on the Gulf Coast. The other was to come down from up North down the Mississippi and get off somewhere near today's Memphis and invade from the West. Of course, without good communications, one army, the one from a French fort up North that came down the Mississippi River, was not there in time. The French general from the Mobile expedition did not want to wait, so he foolishly went ahead and attacked. Everyone, I mean just about everyone on the French side, was wiped out. The general and his staff and even the priest were the few remaining alive and captured. They were quickly staked and burned alive so that the Chickasaws could go through their ritual of eating some flesh of their conquered enemies.

Only a French surgeon escaped, and he ultimately found a couple of runaway Africans. Together they found the other French army coming from the Mississippi River and warned them not to attack. But that army attacked anyway, and they got whipped, too, except the general and a handful of the French were able to escape. The French never challenged the Chickasaw again. And it was during that first battle of Ackia that one of the two gold chalices went missing."

"What happened?"

"Tippahjo only said that the chief, Chief Tanglefoot, as he was preparing to leave this area for the coming battle near today's Tupelo had talked with the Keeper of the Secret and together, they had decided to have the gold chalice present during the battle. I don't know if it was for good luck or what. You know in the Bible there is the story of the Ark of the Covenant being used in battle for the Israeli army to win."

"Yeah, and the one time that Ark was captured, the enemy returned it because it was causing disease and disaster in their city."

"Yep, I know that, but the gold cup used somehow during the battle of Ackia never was found or returned. As far as Tippahjo knew, it was lost. Tippahjo's great-grandfather, Mantachie, was the Keeper of the Secret during that battle of Ackia. He told the Judge that his grandfather never gave details of what happened. He said that the story was that his great-grandfather and the chief, that would be Chief Tanglefoot, never returned. Chief Tanglefoot's battle gear included a headdress of gray feathers from turkeys and hawks. I remember that the Judge vividly described Tippahjo's description of that chief in battle with raccoon-like eyes painted with the circles and black paint in lines like eagle wings from his nose to his ears. His actions were legendary in battle, and he never returned after the Battle of Ackia. Tippahjo's grandfather became the new Keeper of the Secret at a young age.

"Now history recorded that several warriors ran after being shot and wandered around into the woods and died later from gut wounds much like the Chickasaw did when Hernando DeSoto's soldiers shot them 200 hundred years earlier. But when I think of the battle for Ackia, in my mind I always remember the story about Chief Tanglefoot. I can even now just close my eyes and think about those raccoon blackened eyes and the eagle's wings war paint."

"Did anyone ever find Chief Tanglefoot's body and bury him?"

"No, and the Keeper of the Secret, Tippahjo's grandfather, only said that the gold chalice was never found."

"Just like Tanglefoot and Tippahjo's great-grandfather," exclaimed Patrick.

"Whelp, now both are a part of the secret. And you and I must needs get back to work. We probably won't get a full truckload of pulpwood today. There are not as many old scrubby trees and broken tops from the ice storm as I thought there were down here. That's why after the yellowjackets' attack, I figured we needed a good break and that was as good a time as any to initiate you into the family of the Keepers of the Secret."

"Is there anything else that I need to know?" asked Patrick.

"Son, I will tell you some more, but you know just about as much as I do about the secret. In fact, about the secret, you know everything now. That's it. But I never showed you Tippahjo's rain dance, did I?"

"No, Pappy, I never knew that you had a rain dance in you."

"I have on more than one occasion come out here in the dry summer when we needed a rain, and I have performed the dance. Within 24 hours it has rained every time. Now I will admit that the rain might have been just local, not like a huge front coming in, but it has rained every time that I have danced."

"Really?"

"Like I said it might not be some huge threat coming through that rains for hours and days, but even in the summer months we would get a shower."

"Can you show me the dance?"

"Nobody has ever seen me do it, but since you are a future Keeper of the Secret, let me show you before we get back to work. But first, I must find a willow tree around here."

"Why a willow tree?"

"Tippahjo told the Judge that it was connected to the sky like a tree magnet for water vapors. Its leaves and branches droop down because they communicate with their roots in the ground and the willow tree draws energy from the earth and the sky. He said that when you do the rain dance underneath a willow tree that it was like a reverse lightning of some sort. It's not like you might see rain dances in movies and on television. They never seem to know what they are doing. If you want rain to come, first find a wet tree like the willow tree and start underneath it. It's like in baseball, you never get to score unless you first get to base. That's why I always look for a willow tree. I researched this once from a forester from Mississippi State. I asked him why some trees drop sap in the summer from the leaves. He said they call it honeydew, but it's really a bacterial infection of the tree. But the Chickasaws, now they didn't say it had to be a willow tree. It's just that whenever I find a willow tree out here, it is always dripping. But some of your big leaf oaks, like the swamp white oaks and the blackjack oaks, now they would probably do, but I always have used a willow tree when we need rain."

"Well, it's dry now so do you want me to help you go find a willow tree? We could use a little rain; I am sure all the nearby farmers could."

"I know there's one not far from here, just a little bit offn' this ridge going away from the ravine. Now let me think a minute," his Pappy said as he ducked his head into one hand as the other hand grasped his elbow. "Let's go this way."

Mostly pines were planted on the ridge now, but a few hardwoods had grown up among them. Patrick's grandfather walked fast and pointed through some outstretched pine limbs, "There it is."

And Patrick could see those long drooping branches with small slender leaves. As he and his grandfather ducked beneath its outside dangling limbs, he could see like an inner sanctuary, a shade from the Mississippi summer sun. A drop of honeydew landed on his forehead. His grandfather bent down and raised both hands over his head. He started chanting and went into rhythmic circles as his head would rise and fall and then hesitate and head fake and then rise again as the circle increased with an occasional stiff kick and then he dragged his opposite foot to mark the ground. Patrick took in the chanting and the moves under the willow tree. His grandfather stopped and said that same movement is repeated ten times moving in a counterclockwise circle, step out two wide steps and then ten times to the clockwise. Sorta like that Ezekiel thing the Chickasaws did of a circle in a circle or a wheel within a wheel."

"I don't understand, how you get a wheel in a wheel."

"It's like a big clock on the outside and a little clock on the inside. You see, the Judge told me that we think like Europeans. We don't understand rain dances, but they were just part of what the Judge said was ancient knowledge that could be what we might say was like unlocking a combination to a vault. The knowledge is in the sky and earth, and the dances release the blessings. Now we better get to work before it starts raining. Your grandmother is going to want us home by supper time, and we will surely have earned it after those yellowjackets stole the show today. You'll be talking about that for years I bet."

"Is that all there is to it?"

"The rain dances?"

"Yes, the rain dances. If I'm going to be a Keeper of the Secret, then I want to know everything."

"You know just about everything because I've showed you the way of the Chickasaw from everything that the Judge taught me that Tippahjo taught him, and now I just added what you need to know about being the Keeper of the Secret."

"Yeah, but that rain dance. I don't think that I could do it if I had to."

"You saw me---oh, and if you do want some lightning, when you are on the outside ring then you always kick dust into the inner ring as you dance. But that does not mean that you will always get lightning. Judge said that it was just adding a bit of begging so the rain may not come as hard if you don't kick for lightning. Got that."

"Not really. But, yeah, if I had to do it, I could. I really could. Should I dance now so that I can remember better?"

"No, let's get back to work. We can go over it again, later. We will have plenty of time before you have to go to campus for the fall semester. We don't need any rain here until we get those pulpwood logs up on top of this ridge."

"Well, will your dance bring rain?"

"I certainly hope not soon. That's why I didn't do the whole dance. Come on, we better hit it to get done now before it gets late into the afternoon. I never would have taken so long for lunch, and I didn't plan to initiate you today. But that's how this land lives through us; what our plans are, are not necessarily what this land plans to do. The yellowjackets were painful, but that's what told me that today was the day to anoint your future as Keeper of the Secret."

Patrick and his grandfather started walking back to the ridge where they had eaten their lunch. "Oops, one more thing. You remember that little Indian mound on the far side of the other ridge where the east path leads to the bubbling up brook?"

"You mean the brook where you just got water that never runs dry?"

"Yep, same brook but different entrance, that's the one. Where the Indian mound is there ain't no Chickasaw buried there. It was there before the Chickasaw. Now it's not the burial place of the gold chalice because that would be too obvious. But you know about all the bones around there where the animals that feel near death wander there to die. The cows, the bobcats, the possums and raccoons. It's just freaky how they know to come and die right there. Before bears and buffaloes were hunted out, I'm sure they did too. Well, I mentioned this because the place of death high on the hill, well, you know that fountain of youth that Ponce De Leon searched for? Seems like the Indians here before the Chickasaws, the ones that Solomon's sea captain met, well somewhere around here was their special waters, and Tippahjo always thought it was that bubbling brook. But he said that just the water didn't keep you young. It was a combination of something that went with the water and that's why hurting and dying animals wander toward this hill. He said that they could smell the flow of life right here. And I believe wherever Ponce de Leon got that story, it was passed down from the days of Solomon the King! Now—you know everything that I know. And I'll stop here by saying that whenever I am on this land, I am stronger, faster, and I don't know how to explain it, but it's like an extra energy swells up from this land into me."

Neither said a word as they descended back down the North Mississippi rolling hill forest. Patrick grabbed the thermos jug of water, and they walked down the newly battened down trail that the truck had made earlier in its morning trek. Patrick revisited the words that he had just heard. He didn't hear the brush of his boots against the native grasses and forest leaves. He was busy re-hearing the words given for the next Keeper of the Secret. So much, so fast and all these years his Pappy had stayed quiet about the secret: King Solomon, son of the slayer of Goliath, who sent ships out to bring treasures back into Israel in 40 years of peace. And from these Bible heroes, now he was to be a part of a secret established in the days of glory for the land of Israel. How could it be? Patrick pinched the flesh on his arm. It's real, "I'm not dreaming" he thought to himself.

Soon Patrick's grandfather had cranked up the saw once again, and Patrick started loading the pulpwood logs onto the bed of the truck. His grandfather continued to fell the trees, cut off their limbs, and then sectioned them into short stick pulpwood. Patrick caught up quickly and other than dodging a few trees on their way down that Pappy was cutting, he acted almost like a machine. With sticky pine rosin on his gloves and loose bark bits falling from his long sleeves in between his gloves and his hands, he would reach down and whip the little sticks up, but the larger logs he would stand up with the heavier and wider end to the ground and then place it on his leg to position it. He grunted as he carried the wood over briars, bushes, trimmed limbs, and vines, taking the pulpwood to the truck bed piece by piece. The Mississippi heat was now brutal, and every fiber of his pants and shirt were drenched. The only thing fresh now was the smell of fresh cut pine. But with every deep breath and every swipe of the sweat from his forehead, Patrick kept churning the fiery words that his ears had funneled into his brain.

His grandfather stopped to take a break. He, too, was drenched but with sawdust sticking to his sweaty clothes. His grandfather grabbed the water jug, sat down and leaned against the trunk of a wide yellow poplar tree. The few falling yellow leaves from the dry weather floated over Patrick's grandfather as he lifted the water jug to his mouth. After a long drink he said loudly, "Patrick, you better come take a rest. When you get too hot, you and me neither will be worth more than a Buffalo nickel for the rest of the day."

"Pappy, go ahead and rest, but I want to get caught up with the logs you already got cut."

"You won't have many more left after our break so come on and sit down. I only have a few more trees to cut down and saw up."

"Let me go ahead and get these last four logs to the truck. That's all I have left, and then I will be caught up."

"Go ahead son. I need to sharpen the saw blades in a minute anyway."

Patrick continued loading the pulpwood. As he gathered his last stick, he looked over to see his grandfather resting with a peace about him that he had never really noticed before, like a professor in college, well achieved and humble. He deserved a doctorate degree in Native American history. A rest for weary bones he was thinking. His intellect and knowledge of the Chickasaws from memory and handed down stories was incalculable. How many more stories did he have to tell? Hunting in these woods and crawling through these swamps and fields and hills in all seasons came ringing back through his mind, and never had he ever suspected that his grandfather was such a reservoir of knowledge who was walking on this earth unnoticed. Patrick was thinking about all the stories he needed his grandfather to start retelling now that he knew him as the Keeper of the Secret. Land and water and sky now seemed to flow beautifully with everything that Patrick's grandfather had told to him all his life---something spiritual, something true intertwining up from this ground on which he now stood. Something natural ran through his veins; was it that Chickasaw blood now beating through his heart like it always had but with something new? Would he now know something more than he had ever known before when it comes to walking on this land? He wondered what this proclamation and initiation would come to. The sweat and the long, wet sleeves in the Mississippi heat seemed to even cool him as a breeze blew through the trees. He walked over to his grandfather and reached for the jug of water. "Have you really never seen the secret?"

"I've already told you about that. Never seen it and I don't reckon any Keeper of the Secret has except for Tippahjo's great-grandfather. I was told that it was somewhere from the top of that yonder hill and the Hatchie Bottom. That's why to me the top of that hill looks like the head of a pregnant woman."

"I know that you told me when I was little that you could stand on the top of that hill and spit and on one side the rainwater would take it to the Hatchie River and on the other side that the rain would it carry all the way down the Tallahatchie which flows South; and, of course, the Hatchie flows North."

"Yep, you still remember that right. I've always wanted to tell you about the pregnant looking lay of the land but now you know. You got to remember that deep ravine down there," he motioned over to the nearby drop off, "Well, it was only a low place back whenever they decided to bury whatever treasure that they buried besides the two gold chalices. It never turned into this ravaging ravine until the white men cut down the trees and made cotton fields on these rolling hills. Then the deep gully appeared and has gotten so big and washed out that animals don't even try to cross it. They just go into the bottom and walk around it. You can see the deer tracks, and that's the way the wild animals get around it."

"So that tree that fell into the deep ravine, I don't guess you are going to try and salvage any of it for pulpwood."

"Well, you know me well. Now Patrick, you know that I don't usually waste anything. But I know better than to get close to that ledge with my chainsaw. Even if I found some good leverage it's just too dangerous. You know how good I am with a chainsaw, and that is why I 've never had a bad accident. Better safe than sorry even though you know that I hate to get beat and I hate not to fully utilize everything. Don't like to waste nothing. My parents lived through the Great Depression, and they told me about having to eat possums and Hoover rabbits. They never wasted nothing."

"I've always known how good you are with a chainsaw. I've seen you cut trees down by lifting that chainsaw above your shoulders so that you could get the right angle. I didn't think you were really all that safe when you were cutting like that."

"Well don't go and tell your grandmother that I ever do things like that. She always wants to make sure I get back home every time I come out here. When I used to coon hunt at night, now she never got used to that. I had to have some of my hunting buddies talk to her and soothe her fears down."

"Did you ever see anything around here when you were coon hunting at night?"

"Well, we coon hunted all over; but being the Keeper of the Secret, I always for some reason just protected this area because, well, I really don't know why, but just like the Keeper of the Secret felt about Hernando DeSoto, I just don't want anyone getting near here on my watch. That's why you don't know this ravine area as well. I always told you that I didn't want you to fall off into it and that snakes are all around here, but really I just always felt like I was more like a protector, and you don't have to protect what no one is milling about."

"We don't have that much left to get finished, do we?"

"Nope, I just need to cut down those four or five trees; and when you get them loaded up, then we will head for home. When it starts getting a shade darker after the sun goes down below the upper ridge, I'm telling you that there are times in the past that I felt like Bigfoot or someone or something was down here watching me. I could feel eyes just staring right into my back. Whenever I turned around really quick, all I ever could see were more woods. I'm tellin' you if you were a movie producer and you wanted to do a haunted movie, then just build a house in these woods and you would have the actors' hairs standing straight up by just hearing the bobcats and the coyotes and all kinds of animals a hollering in these woods. And I'm saying that in the late afternoon; I don't just mean at midnight. You see these dense woods down in these hollers can get like a jungle. Now I've never been to a jungle you see on television, but I can't imagine much denser, thicker vines and trees and canopies and swamps and cypress trees and knees and quicksand and sandbars and creeks and channels and snakes and wild varmints than what we have down in these Hatchie Bottom lands."

"Well, I was about to say that while you start cutting those last trees, I was going to go and inspect that tree that fell into the deep ravine, but you just about made me scared just to go exploring down there, Pappy." Patrick smiled a grin that meant that he was up to something mischievous.

"Oh," his grandfather said laughing a little, "If you were just a few years younger, I could have you really scared. Go ahead and take a look; you are the next Keeper of the Secret. Just be careful and don't stir up anymore yellowjackets and don't fall and break a leg or something bad like that."

Patrick walked over to where the tree he and his grandfather had tried to push away from the ravine still lay with only its wide butt trunk sticking up from the ravine near its stump. During the spectacle when he and his grandfather had failed to push the tree in their desired trajectory, Patrick had not had time to even look into the deep ravine much less investigate it. As he approached the ravine, he looked at the trunk of the tree and felt like a soldier looking at a vanquished foe. Now he more than identified with the fallen tree. He looked back to his grandfather and thought of how he had said it hurt to remove the trees. For the first time he thought he saw a glimpse of what his grandfather was seeing when the trees he cut changed the scenery of what he knew. Patrick thought back to when he had heard his grandfather say that in his early years, he saw the cotton fields on the hills and the hardwoods filled only the bottom lands and stretches where the hills were too steep to farm. He remembered how his grandfather once said that as these fields slowly were planted into pine, that as the trees retook the hills, that now it was getting closer to what the land was like when the

Chickasaws once roamed free. And as he cut down the scrubby, less valuable trees to make way for the saw logs to grow and increase in value, he was, in a way, not protecting the land like he would like. Oh, thought Patrick, but he justifies the cutting because he controls the land somewhat even though he is not the owner. But he is the Keeper of the Secret and if he (Patrick) now was also training to be the Keeper of the Secret, was his aiding in removing the massacred trees a way to be introduced to bonding with the land? Would this land rebel? Could this land that was returning somewhat to what it was once before now able to reverse and throw back everything that the "civilized" world had done to tame it like taming a wild horse? The Hatchie River had its tributary creeks and channels like the Little Hatchie River carved out by machines and man so that the almost annual flooding was better contained for more farmland and crops and more money and taxes. For all that changing the hills had not changed their rolling ridges, only the deep gullies and ravines that man had squandered with decades of topsoil erosion that washed off these foothills of the Appalachian Mountains. And now Patrick knew something that he had never known before. He couldn't put his finger on it, he couldn't explain it to anyone if they asked, but he knew he was in a midst of change. Now he peered into the deep of the abyss. He was in the bottomland and now there was a deeper ravine that edged itself into the swamps that were between the bottom and the Little Hatchie that flowed into the Hatchie River. Patrick was about to start his descent into the red dirt abyss when he suddenly turned toward his grandfather to shout out. "Pappy, tell me why you're doing this; is it worth it? I mean look at your life. You've been stuck here guarding this land and for what?" Patrick's voice shouted over the cut down trees and the severed limbs forward to what was left of the trees—-their limbless trunks chopped on the bed of the truck.

"What did you say, son?"

"I said why? What makes your life worth it? All of this. It has kept you tied to this land your whole life. And for what?"

"Well, son, I've lived a good life. Never had much money, but I have loved every day on this earth. Me and your grandmother, now we have our needs met. We have two healthy children and three fine grandkids. I have taken you fishing, and hunting, and we have entertained ourselves quite well here, haven't we? You were my only male grandkid, and now you're going to be the next Keeper of the Secret."

"Yeah, but Pappy, where does it take you? Where will it take me? Now I want to go see the world. I have been to California and New York City. I want to go to Europe. Christine, she's from Germany. I want to meet her family."

"Ahhh, yes. Christine. She has changed your life in a way."

"In a big way. If we get married, and I don't know if that's in the picture just yet, but now she has dreams of living in these big cities and how can I be the Keeper of the Secret if I am in New York City? What if Christine wants to visit back in Germany, and what if we don't live around here?"

"Whoa, son. You are going too fast. First, you have to know that this land chooses you."

"I don't know what you mean?"

"In a way you must feel these interaction signals that I can feel when I walk these hills."

"Signals?"

"Yes, vibrations that are like a buzzing sound, like trying to find a radio station, and it's that fuzz factor---not sound as much as a vibration that echoes throughout these hills, and I know it, but it has only come over the years of being here. I never knew it at a young age, even when the Judge made me Keeper of the Secret. It was another ten to fifteen years before I started to hear or feel these vibrations. It's like I have learned to tune into these signals like you would use a radio to listen to different stations."

"Like what kind of vibrations?"

"Like the land was trying to speak or wanted to move or shake or nudge me forward."

"What does that have to do about me and my future?"

"That's what I am trying to tell you. This land calls out, and deep inside I want to answer by protecting, guarding, and just standing watch."

"Will I want to come here when say I am visiting New York City and in all the noise and traffic and people by the thousands walking by? Do you think I will somehow hear a buzzing calling me back to this land of the Chickasaws like some kind of bat signal to Batman?"

"I dunno. But we are working here getting these trees removed to make better sawlogs for the Judge's son and to make money for your going to college. That is a win-win situation. And if this land on which we are working and protecting allows you to go to college and then someday say go to New York City and live. Well, then, this land will somehow by faith connect to you, and you will know when you need to come back and that I think is the buzzing vibration that you will in time understand and it will communicate with you. It's like when we are hunting with all the sounds of the hills and bottoms with the birds and the crickets and the cicadas along with the mud sucking sound as you lift your boot up from the swampy soil of half-decayed leaves and the mush sound of your other foot coming back down. Now these sounds of the breaking sticks and the limbs slapping back all in unison together I believe tie the past and the future. That is the buzzing that I know, and it is like a lifeline that even when I am home, I concentrate and I know it's still going on and it connects me. If it connects me, it will one day connect you and you will know. Just like King Solomon knew about these lands, and around the world this land must beat like a heartbeat, and it is truly a pathway as surely as the Natchez Trace connected lands and peoples so long ago. And there is nowhere on this earth that you can go and not hear what is in this land because this land is in you. And from here you can go anywhere."

Patrick stood before his grandfather holding one elbow and with his chin resting in the other hand. He was contemplating all these words he had just heard. In his mind he wanted to believe his grandfather, but, in his heart, there was doubt. "I've never heard this land buzz. Where the power company has those huge connecting towers and we walk underneath, I can hear and feel that buzz."

"Yes, I've not thought about that. It is similar."

"I just don't know how I can be Keeper of the Secret and live a long way from here?"

"Trust me, you will know."

"You should know. I guess that I have a lot to learn now."

"You do have a lot to learn but you won't be learning it from me. I've told you everything that I know."

"Where's the gold cup from the Battle of Akcia, with the French?"

"I don't know. Like I said, you now know everything. Oh, you will learn but it will be you coming here by yourself, walking, coming here in a thunderstorm and watching how the water flows down these hills and fills up the creeks and seeing where the overflows go."

"I can guess where a lot of water goes. Right down this ravine."

"You got that right."

"O.K. then. I'm going to do that exploring a little while you get these other trees cut."

Patrick was not wanting to hear any buzz of yellowjackets, but he was wondering, how does this land vibrate if it's not even moving? Can this land be alive? Patrick looked to where a large limb near the trunk of the tree had dug into the red dirt sides of the deep ravine. The yellowjackets had calmed down. A few could be seen lightly buzzing in a non-aggressive nature, trying to repair their home in the side of the red dirt wall positioned near the top of the red wall just underneath some overgrowth tree roots that provided shelter from the rain. Patrick slipped over to the other side of the trunk where there were no yellowjackets. He eased down the side of the steep drop off by hanging on to the fallen tree. He shimmered down the limbs of the tree as if he were in an upside-down treehouse. He lowered himself into the deep gully. He thought to himself that these limbs were like hands from people helping him down toward the gully floor where some sandstones were naturally spread by periodic storms in the dry red sand that was left from the last big rain that had flooded through the ravine. The top of the tree was near the bottom of the gully, and its heavy green pine limbs were thick against the side of the red walls. And midway down he saw a flash of light, a glint---just a glint that caused him to pause. He reached to move some of the green pine needles and the light was shining like a yellow bright flashlight beam. The beam was like a powerful battery backed charged light with brilliance. It was coming from a black hole below the green pine top limbs. It was as if the limbs were not resting on the red dirt, but one side of the tree limbs was hanging freely in the dark of the small black hole. Patrick reached to try and pull the tree limbs up so that he could get a better view. As he did the flashlight-like beam disappeared as the pine brush blocked the sun from reflecting on what was below. It surprised him and perplexed his brain simultaneously as his head raced to take it in.

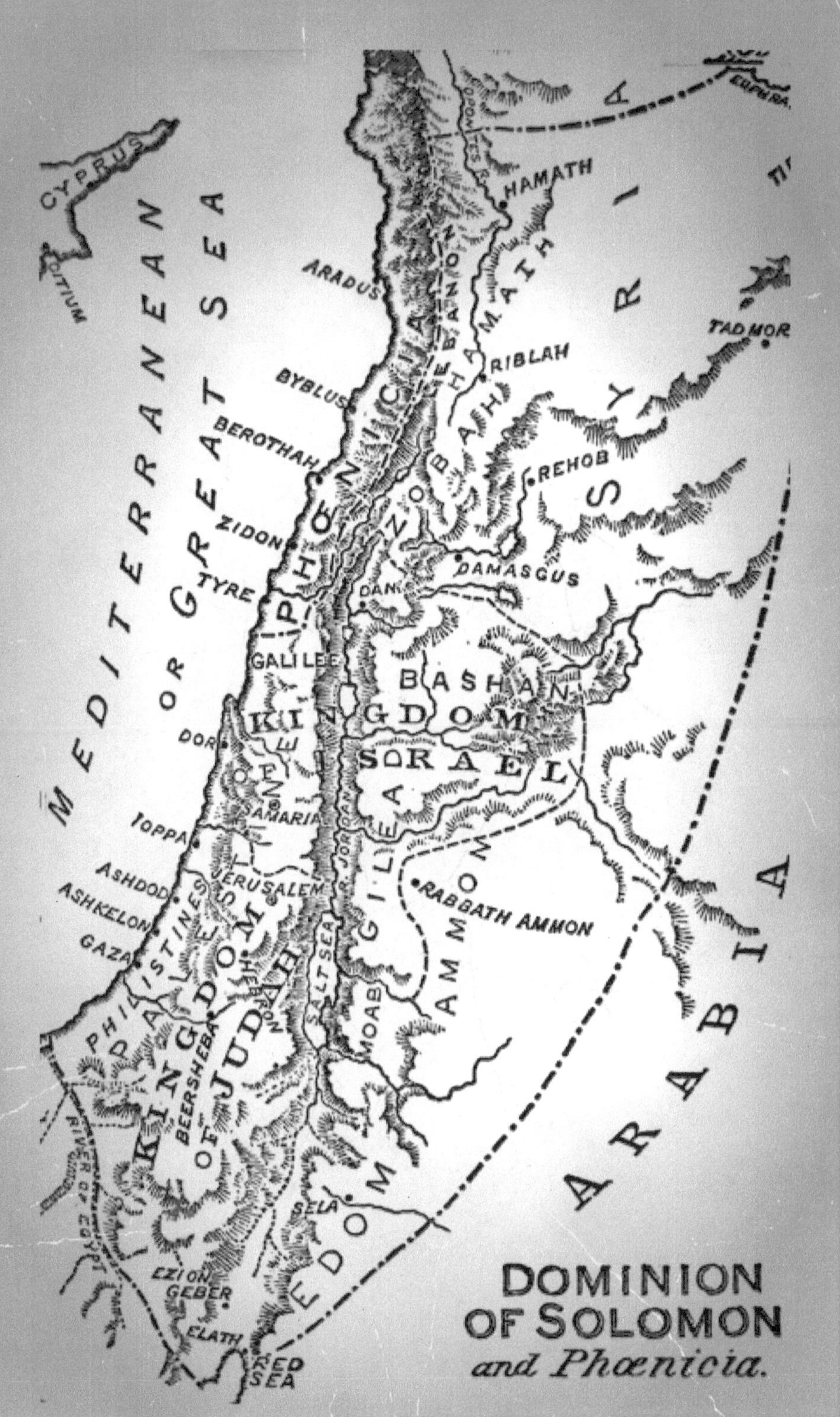

DOMINION OF SOLOMON *and Phœnicia.*

Chapter 4

Patrick was now driven. He was the explorer. He was the tip of the spear in a new investigation and with a new historical perspective. He had just seen a light that just disappeared. He was mystified. Once again, he moved the limb enough to see the golden sunlight reflected to him in brilliance and power. Patrick looked to see the sun still above the tree line of the ridge, but it was nearing that severance point where it would soon disappear. It would be full daylight only for a few more minutes as the golden beams of the sun flared back in a mirrored beam full of wonder. A rich reflection deep, thick, lush, powerful all together like nothing he had ever seen or even imagined. It was deep down in that black hole as if there was a chamber that the pine limb had crashed through. Patrick's thoughts suddenly reached back to ancient Egypt and the pyramids and the pharaohs and to mummies and burial chambers. What was this?

Patrick wanted to shout, but his voice was muted in frozen muscle excitement. His eyes stared in disbelief. His ears sought sound, but there was no sound, no voice, no smell or touch for a moment, just his eyes locked onto that shining light beaming up from an object reflecting the sunlight as if it were a floating lamp... a golden floating lamp in a sea of darkness. What could this be? Was this the secret? Was he now seeing what so few had known about but had never seen? Is this the treasure that DeSoto sought? What should he do?

Wanting to shout to his grandfather but with his voice frozen, he just moved forward, breathless to peer into the black hole with its resplendent light jumping, pumping its spell into his face like a magnet pulling him closer. He brushed back the pine limbs from the tree. The hole was just wide enough to drop or crawl into. Would he drop to a floor? His brain was automatically weighing his choices about how to quickly get into that hole. The beam drew him forward. He grabbed the lesser-sized but stable trunk towards the top of the tree. And like hanging or dangling from a bar, he then dropped his feet into the hole. Before he could think, his feet were descending into the opening, then his waist and his shoulders and he had not reached a floor. Surely, he thought for an instant that if that flash of reflection were near, then the floor of this chamber could not be too far away. As he released, he fell to a brick-like floor. Then he saw it. He saw the golden beam source reflecting from the inside of a gold chalice lying upon a table but not just any table, but a table carved of elaborate carvings like some wooden splendor from a novel. And now he could see behind the table was an entire wall of gold pieces. Not gold bars like he had seen in pictures of Fort Knox but a wall of round bracelets of gold dangling in ordered fashion together like circles of chains and gold squares and rings of gold. This is the mother lode he thought. This, this is what Hernando DeSoto sought!

Patrick approached the shining chalice and stopped amid great reverence and respect. He gazed at its beauty and fine design from expert craftsmen. These details were crafted by men mentioned in the Old Testament. His heart kept beating, but his limbs were frozen and would not move as if his body were oblivious to all that was now around him. His eyes stayed focused on the chalice. The golden beam toned itself down, and the glow began to fade as Patrick knew that the sun was going down below the tree line on the high ridge and the wall of gold brilliance behind the table now weakened. Wow and wow and how! But now all he wanted to do was go and show the Keeper of the Secret that he was right, and the treasure was here! The treasure was right here where the pregnant land was like an Indian princess with the treasure stored in her womb. He thought of the word tomb, rhyming with womb, and he thought back to his previous visions of the ancient mummies and pyramid tombs. This was not a tomb but more like an ancient bank of treasures from ages long ago and peoples who were not stone age by any means. The chamber was dry and sealed with some kind of concrete-like paste of a mud plaster. The chamber had sat here unmolested until the pine tree's force from its fall blew a hole through the rain-eroded topsoil of the secret chamber.

The inner chamber's floor was thick like solid concrete. Whatever the ancients had used, it was certainly sturdy material that stood the test of time. Patrick was still in awe of it all. He watched as the reflected gold beam continued to fade and the brightness of all the gold objects behind the stately table continued to fade. He regained his muted voice and started yelling, "Pappy! Pappy! Come quick.!" But he could hear the chainsaw still cutting through pine. He immediately decided to get back out of the chamber to go and tell his grandfather, but instantly and without thinking his hand stretched out to retrieve the golden chalice. He grabbed the table on which the chalice had stood to move it underneath the hole from which he had just entered. The table was tremendously heavy, about four feet wide and just two feet across the top of the table. Patrick wondered what kind of wood from which this ancient table was made. It was stout and heavy and difficult to move, but he needed its height to get back through the small hole. After dragging the table across the chamber floor, he steadied himself and reached with one hand to grab the tree trunk still over the hole and held on to the chalice with his other hand. He started to pull himself up, but even with his workout routines he could not manage to get out using just one arm. He threw the gold chalice through the hole and heard it hit outside and roll. He used both hands to pull himself out of the chamber and then went to retrieve the golden cup.

He could not see the chalice anywhere. He knew that it had rolled because he heard it roll after he pitched it up and through the hole. The treetop was draped over the entire length of the slope of the ravine. But its top was near the bottom with its trunk still standing where the ravine began near its stump on the grassy ground at the surface. Patrick was instantly desperate not only to find the chalice, but as a future Keeper of the Secret he now felt entirely responsible for the treasures in that chamber. He had just held the golden chalice and now it was gone. He frantically lifted the treetop looking beneath it. Nothing but sandstone and red dirt sand. He looked up at the entirety of the tree. He surveyed, and yet nowhere could he see a gold cup.

For the first time he noticed that not only had the sun started to descend behind the ridge of trees so high up from this deep pit of the gully, but overhead dark clouds were forming, too. That Mississippi summer humidity was being swept away by a cool swift breeze that comes before a thunderstorm---one that promised to be a gullywasher, no doubt. With dread of the disappearance of the cup and now the imminent storm approaching, he knew that he and his grandfather had to get the load of wood out of the low place before the rain started.

"Patrick! Son! Come on and help me get these last few sticks loaded. We gotta get out of here quick!"

"Pappy!"

"What?"

"Pappy! It's here!" Patrick's voice was different, and his grandfather knew it with the celebratory accentuated pronouncement.

"What's here?"

"The secret! The treasure! The tree that tore into the yellowjacket's nest also knocked a hole into the secret treasure chamber!"

Patrick's grandfather's feet started running to the ravine. As he got to the edge, he dropped his feet over the edge of the ravine and held on to the trunk in midair at the top of the ravine. "God Almighty!"

"Be careful, Pappy! Don't want you to fall and break a leg," Patrick said with concern because he could tell that his grandfather's feet were moving with the same quickness that had caused him to outrun Patrick up to the top of the hill earlier when the yellowjackets had attacked. His grandfather was thin but stout and strong, and he held tightly to the downed tree branches as gravity and his weight dropped him quickly. He descended until he was eyeball to eyeball with his grandson.

"Where?"

Patrick pointed to the hole and now with the darkening skies and the sun going down there was no reflection of gold that

Patrick had seen earlier. "I saw it when the sun reflected the light back from the gold!"

"How much gold?"

"Lots!"

"I can't see it from here."

"I will run back to the truck and get the flashlight from the emergency kit."

"Good thinking." Patrick's grandfather was smiling, breathing hard because he was out of breath with excitement. It had been a hard-working day, but he was not going to miss this for anything. Far off in the distance lightning flashed.

Patrick was now at the top of the ravine. He saw the lightning and knew that he needed to get to the truck fast. Then they would have to hurry, or they would never drive that truck with its logs up the steep wet incline to get back to the logging road on the ridge above. Then he heard it for the first time ever. The shrieking howl of horror. A wolf's howl? His grandfather looked up, disturbed.

"Do you see anything?" his grandfather shouted with fear in his voice.

"No. But did you hear that?"

"That was the howl of a wolf or some godforsaken creature!"

"I thought that there were no wolves anywhere around here."

"They're not."

"Then what was that?"

"It's a wolf, I think. There used to be bunches of them when the Chickasaw were here. But it sounds more like a cat cry. Might not be a wolf. The tall tales in this whole land of secrets is that black panthers once roamed here."

Patrick asked, "What should we do?" He looked up to the darkening sky to see that the far-off lightning was getting closer. He saw a flash and then counted, "One Mississippi, two Mississippi, three Mississippi." Then the thunder roared and shook the earth.

His grandfather saw the same thing and quickly summed up the information and said, "Let me get up out of here and let's reassess. I'm not leaving here with that hole there though. It will be covered up before I ever leave here!" He struggled to pull himself up the steep ravine by pulling up on the trunk of the fallen pine just as Patrick had done. But he was sweating hard, grunting with deep breaths.

Patrick was surveying the situation from the top of the ravine and was looking up the second steep incline towards the ridge. He felt that he was in a large deep well with his grandfather stuck even deeper in a cave of some sort. He turned his head to look where he had heard the howling sound. And he saw nothing but the dark clouds swarming and swirling with the grays and the deep blue clouds intertwining as fronts weaved in and out with smooth ferocity that sparked the lightning bolts. He looked back down as his grandfather continued to climb. Patrick was nervous. "Do you need some help down there?"

"Lot harder than it was coming down! I didn't say anything but somehow, I turned my ankle in the descent."

"Always harder climbing out. Do you want me to come down there and help you up?"

"Normally I would say no, but we need to get out of the ravine so that we can decide what to do fast!"

"I agree," said Patrick as he grabbed back on to the trunk of the tree at the ravine's top. The thought crossed his mind that he was going down the trunk at the top of the ravine so that he could get to the top of the tree deep down in the gully. He made his way down to where his grandfather had just struggled a few feet up from where the hole was in the chamber. It was getting darker, and now Patrick could not even see the hole, but he knew where it was. He grasped the trunk hard and reached down to his grandfather and said, "Here, grab my hand and I will help you up."

His grandfather grabbed his hand and Patrick pulled up. He stopped each step with his boots kicked into the red dirt wall and one hand and arm grasping the trunk of the pine and the other hand pulling his grandfather up. His grandfather was still huffing and puffing, breathing hard but saying nothing with a worried look on his face. They both heard the piercing shriek again.

"Could that really be a wolf howl?"

"Let me get to the top, and I will tell you then."

Once again Patrick struggled up the tree helping his grandfather along the way. As they reached the top of the ravine, Patrick leaped over to the solid ground, then reached down to pull his grandfather to the top. "Let's rest a minute, son." They both sat down on the ground with the screeching wind picking up, but no rain or even a sprinkle had fallen. Patrick looked over to his grandfather to see his chest moving in and out breathing hard, sweating. He was thinking, "I'm glad we can rest a moment."

Suddenly his grandfather popped up and cried out, "No time to rest! Let's go!" He started running toward the truck.

"What is it?" Patrick called out as he jumped up in pursuit.

The Table of Shewbread.
EXOD.XXV. 23.30.
EXOD.XXIV. 5. 6.
The Altar of Incense.
EXOD.XXX.1. 5.
The Candlestick.
EXOD.XXV.31.37.
The Censer.
The Altar of Brass in Solomons Temple
2. CHRON. IV. 1.
The Ark of the Covenant with the mercy seat.
EXOD. XXV. 10.21.
One of the ten brazen lavers in Solomons Temple standing on its base or pedestal.
I. KINGS VII. 27. 38.

Chapter 5

"Panthers!" His grandfather cried out pointing across the ravine. "A pack of panthers!"

"Where did they come from?"

"Swamp panthers from deep in the Hatchie Bottom. I knew that they still existed!" His grandfather said, puffing as he ran.

"What are we going to do?"

"That ravine seems to have them stopped for the moment. Maybe they don't think they can get up that steep wall."

"I hope that they didn't see us climb up that fallen tree."

Patrick's grandfather motioned to follow him. He ran back to the butt end of the tree they had just climbed up the steep red dirt wall. "Help me push it into the bottom of the ravine!" Together they shoved the butt end enough so that its weight gained momentum and the entire tree slid down the dirt wall and rolled into the deep bottom of the ravine. His grandfather ran back to the chainsaw, stooped down on the run and grabbed the chainsaw. "I just sharpened the blades before I got those last few trees cut down."

"Let me carry it, Pappy!"

"Ok," he said, handing the chainsaw over to Patrick as they looked like sprinters in a track and field race passing a very big baton.

His grandfather leaped over a pine branch sticking up. Patrick jumped with the chainsaw but did not clear the branch and fell face first to the ground. "Shittim Bottom, that hurts! That blade is sharp!"

"Are you ok?"

"Yes, just cut through my britches with those sharp blade teeth, I think."

"Here they come!" His grandfather hollered with a rising tone.

"What?" But Patrick knew as soon as the words were leaving his lips. He glanced as he lay horizontal on the ground to see and hear and even smell all at once the panthers' heads popping up over the edge of the ravine as their legs were fast digging on the steep dirt wall. They were digging in for traction to gain the edge of the ledge. He could simultaneously see a head pop and cat howl and fall back below the ravine edge as another panther with ears cocked back and teeth snarling, cried out a shriek like a woman being attacked.

His grandfather grabbed the chainsaw and ran toward the truck. Patrick was right behind him. Two panthers made it over the ledge and were now in motion running towards the truck. "We gotta get in the truck now! " shouted Patrick's grandfather. In one sweeping motion he yelled these words toward Patrick, turning his head to make eye contact with Patrick but what he saw pierced his soul. These were black panthers of the old tales, large, demonic, vicious, evil in every way representing the Prince of Darkness. Fear stunned his grandfather, but Patrick was too young to fear that deeply. These panthers were gaining fast, and they both knew that they could not make it to the truck in time. Instinctively Patrick's grandfather grabbed the handle to the cord to crank the chainsaw's engine. He felt the warmth of the just used engine and knew that the chainsaw should fire up fast---and it did. With puffs of smoke surrounding him and Patrick, they blended into the dark scene of evil all around. It was just one more dark sight in the circle of evil with the deep gray sky and the blustery wind sending dead leaves flying amongst the lightning flashes and the ground shaking thunder rolls.

Patrick thought back to the black hole and what he saw as he crawled through that hole and the gold chalice. "Where did it go? What have I awakened? What have I done? Every evil spirit and demon seems to have been unleashed," he thought, "and now we are going to die. I am with the Keeper of the Secret, and this land must help us now." Everything that could be used for protection was in the truck thought Patrick. The first panther lunged at his grandfather, but the chainsaw blade running hot met the panther dead center of the panther's nose and just like it was in slow motion there was this awesome splintering of raw nature from a horror movie scene, and then it was blood splattering the air with panther teeth and flesh flying and the insurgent shrieking from hell that smothered to a whimper as the chainsaw cut into the panther's throat. The wild guttural cry diminished to a muffled whimper and then nothing against the bloody chainsaw. Patrick stood frozen next to the first panther's body when he saw the second panther going for his grandfather's back. Instinctively he grabbed a smaller stick of pulpwood from the ground by its smaller end, and swinging the stick with all his might, he smote the fiend square in the head. He watched the big black cat roll to the ground momentarily. Then the panther sprang right back up, but it gave his grandfather enough time to turn around with the chainsaw blazing its metal teeth into the heart and belly of the dark fiend. A third panther pranced straight toward them, not delayed at all by the first two panthers' fates. His grandfather went straight to the jugular. With the machine's teeth blazing and blood flying once again, the chainsaw won quickly and effectively. Just as Patrick smiled a smile of relief, there was no time because he shouted,

"Watch out, Pappy!" as he pointed to the ravine and five more panthers were popped up over the edge.

Still not enough time to get in the truck and with the panthers on the run, Patrick's grandfather gassed the chainsaw and stood like a soldier with a flashing bayonet. The panthers came strong with one purpose, to kill! With the dead first wave of panthers lying mangled before them and the smell of smoke and gas and blood all mixed in the air, it was war deep in the valley of death now. Patrick jumped onto the loaded logs on the back of the truck as his grandfather stood stiff like a concrete statue of a soldier defending his land, his chainsaw not still as its rotating teeth were fiercely circling fast and ready to kill again. Patrick grabbed another log and just chunked it over his grandfather's head where it came down on the first of the pack. It slowed the leader down just enough so the second panther bought the ticket for his face to meet his grandfather's chainsaw blades. Once again, the panther's head was first to meet the ripping blades, but this time it was right down the middle of the panther's head. This time the panther flinched and turned its head so that the eye and ear were separated just before the brain tissue came spinning out. As it fell to the feet of Patrick's grandfather, the first panther, which had been hit by the log came back up to jump his grandfather with a ferocity that knocked him down. Patrick went straight into action heaving down a stick of wood like a spear into the side of the panther. His grandfather returned to his feet, gassed the saw just in time for panther number three of the second wave. And that is when the torrential rain started pouring down so thick that Patrick could not see his grandfather. It was chilled and dark, and he could hear the chainsaw grinding and panthers shrieking and then their whimpers before death. Just then the lightning flash showed his grandfather was on the ground cutting into one of the panthers with the chainsaw as another panther was tearing into the flesh of his shoulder.

Patrick jumped down with a pulpwood log in his hand ready to pound the beast, but the flash of lightning was gone, and the thunder rattled the entire land like vocal cords vibrating with a breath blowing out from the fiend lungs of a giant beast in hell. With the wind whipping and the rain ripping the thick air, Patrick's eyes were fighting the wet running film over his face. He thought this must be hell without the heat and flames. Lightning sizzle-struck the earth, a large tree burst with a cracking boom as sparks and splinters exploded and a fireball emerged. Years of slow growth wood were sheered apart in the twinkling of an eye, and then Patrick felt the heat and saw the flames. When he saw the panther's new position ready to pounce, he thought now this is hell. Helpless in one instance of time, now he immediately felt destiny with his internal flight-or-fight adrenaline kicking in. He knew a new courage was throbbing throughout his arteries in this battle with hellish black panthers that suddenly reminded him of Daniel in the lion's den. But these big cats didn't have their mouths tamed nor their paws. These flesh-ripping giant cats were trying to kill his grandfather and him. He heard the horrid shriek of another panther and his grandfather wail out in pain amongst the chainsaw's grinding; then the panther's shriek snuffled into silence. The nearby panther sprang at Patrick as his lifted log crashed into the panther's back. Patrick heard a crack like a backbone gone, but the cat still moved its head forward enough for Patrick to smell its stinking breath. When Patrick thought he might feel the sting of the nasty fanged teeth on his throat, he saw the cat's eyes fade much like the golden light did as the sun went down on the gold cup that he had seen earlier. Through the driving rain he had not noticed that his grandfather had moved toward him, and now the roaring engine of the chainsaw had powered the blade to sever the panther into two separate pieces. Pappy's adrenaline was pumping through his arteries, too. Now Patrick, who had never heard his grandfather use any foul language, listened with half-shock and half-exhilarating appreciation as the Keeper of the Secret ripped off a line of profanities ending with, "Die you devil-bastard!"

Even with the panther dead Patrick's grandfather kept cutting to decapitate the dead panther. As the head of the panther rolled away the grandfather fell forward onto the severed pieces of panther. Pappy rolled back over to face Patrick with obvious fear and pain in the driving rain. He pulled both hands over his chest and in stuttered words he muttered, "I-I can't breathe. My-my chest feels like it's being crushed."

Then his grandfather went limp as new lightning lit up the surreal scene to show Patrick the pooling blood from where a panther had taken a bite of flesh through his grandfather's work shirt into the shoulder of his grandfather.

"Pappy!" Pappy!"

Patrick shouted as he instinctively looked for more panthers. But as the lightning flashed again and hit another nearby tree, Patrick dove into the wet ground next to his grandfather. Rain still pelted them hard and fast, but now hail came down, pounding his body and making the metal truck rattle. He looked up as another flash of lightning struck. He could see another panther on top of the cab staring into Patrick's face, and it had the high ground amongst the hail and rain.

Replacing fear with a bold courage, Patrick grabbed the chainsaw with its motor still running. Patrick climbed onto the back of the truck, never taking his eyes off the black panther. The chainsaw was heavy, and he had only used a chainsaw cutting a couple of trees in his yard. The steel teeth dripped red with blood, panther flesh and white bone chips refined as if in a blender. Serious business, Patrick drew near the panther still atop of the cab. He was thinking that he had to finish off the panther and start CPR quick. Then he needed to get his grandfather out of there and to a doctor. Pappy's having a heart attack.

The panther wasted no time as Patrick approached walking on the ice balls on top of the logs on the bed of the truck. This panther did not attack straight on but tried to lunge from Patrick's left side. Patrick gassed the saw and the blade tore into the panther's left shoulder--the blade locking up in the bone and sinews. The panther fell off the edge of the loaded wood and to the ground, pulling the chainsaw from Patrick's hands as it was still entangled in the panther's left shoulder above its front left leg. Chainsaw and big cat thumped the ground. Patrick noticed that the rain was nothing more than a drizzle now. The dark clouds were moving on, and in the sunset horizon an orange-red, blood-like sky lay beneath a full white moon beaming its reflecting sun's rays. Patrick grabbed another log of pulpwood as a weapon and remembered the tales he had been told as a kid of a sheriff not far away called Buford Pusser. Here is my Buford stick, he thought, as he jumped to the ground swinging the butt end toward the panther's head. The panther, with super powered strength, jumped up with its left side slumped with the weight of the entangled chainsaw and useless front left leg. Patrick had never laid eyes on another set of eyes, eyeball to eyeball, that appeared so evil and bent on destruction and ready to fight-to-the death. As the panther leaped into the air with chainsaw and all vigor, Patrick was like "Casey at bat." The panther, chainsaw and all, came toward Patrick like a slow-pitched softball, and he swung his bat like Hank Aaron. So vicious was the swinging hit that the chainsaw fell to the ground as the panther went flying ten feet away from the truck, its body snapping against a large tree. Patrick wasted no time to emulate what his grandfather had just done as he reached for the stalled chainsaw and cranked it back up and decapitated the panther from hell. Patrick did not want an injured panther coming back around as he attempted CPR on his grandfather.

The storm had stopped, the full moon and stars present in the sky. Patrick took that as an omen. He looked at his grandfather. In the moonlight he appeared ashen, but was it just the moonlight?

His grandfather's chest was moving, and Patrick could see blood flowing from the wound. I hope that means that his heart is still beating Patrick thought. His grandfather's face was drenched with beads of rain and sweat. He was still bleeding from his shoulder, and he had that white ashen look, but was it fever sweat or just rain? The hail was melting away and huge drops of accumulated rain dripped from the trees. Patrick reached down to lift his grandfather into his arms and pulled him with his boots dragging the ground into the truck's cab that they had not managed to get to when the panthers first attacked them.

Patrick laid him down on the long seat and shut the doors. Just for good measure he locked the doors against whatever else might be lurking or even Lucifer himself.

Chapter 6

His grandfather was looking pale green and clammy. Sweat beads were on his forehead. "What did the gold chalice look like?"

"I've got to get you to a doctor quick!"

His grandfather's voice came back weak and frail. He was exhausted, bleeding, in pain, and his chest was hurting with his struggling breath, but his words did not change, "What did the gold chalice look like?"

Patrick with rain and sweat and panther blood and guts and bone chips dripping and dangling from his face said, "It was round and a thick gold cup sturdy with a firm base, like a trophy-shaped cup base but with handles on two sides. Intricate designs around the lip of the cup and all over the base of the cup. I wished that I could have taken a picture. Between the lip and the base were two leaves connecting the base to the lip. Intricate detailed leaves, maybe like palm branches or something. I've never seen anything like it, pertneer gorgeous to the max and heavy. And I just tossed it out of the chamber so that I could get two hands to grip and pull myself out. I never could find it, and then we heard the panther screams. Do you want me to try and find it now?"

His grandfather shook his head no and whispered, 'No." His voice dry and weak still. "My chest feels like a boulder is pressing down on it and it hurts something awful. I can hardly get my breath. Let's get to a doctor." Then he cracked a little smile and just said, "I wish that I could have seen it."

Patrick pushed hard on the clutch, turned the ignition key and small puffs of exhaust flew up into the cab from the little hole in the floorboard. Patrick hit the accelerator and let off the clutch cumbersomely and the log truck shook and stammered then started to move forward. But just a few feet up the hill, the back tires started to spin. Mud began to sling, even hitting the outside side mirrors. It was all dark now and the only things Patrick could see were the trees in front of him where the headlights illuminated his way. As Patrick pushed the pedal all the way down the engine roared and the back of the truck swiveled slightly to the left and then to the right, but the front tires did not move as the back tires continued to spin. The exhaust was blowing out smoke so much that it engulfed the outside windshield from behind. Clouds of smoke came from above the cab and began to roll down and block Patrick's vision. He heard his grandfather moan in pain.

"Stop son, you're just making the tires dig a deeper rut."

Patrick let off the accelerator and the roar of the engine quietened down, "We've gotta get out of here. Do you think more panthers are out there?"

"Only God knows what might be out there now."

"Do I need to get out and put some of those cut pine limbs under the back tires?" Patrick knew what he needed to do, but he didn't want to get back out into the darkness where he had met the ambassadors of the devil more than once already. Evil had foreshadowed one fight, and he did not want to have a second fight with whatever principalities and dark forces were lurking on this land now. Demons he was thinking, I have fought with the demons, and we are stuck down in the hollow. My grandfather needs a doctor, and he cannot help me now. Lord, Jesus, I need you now; he was thinking and praying as he thought.

"Back it up a little first." Those were all the words his grandfather now managed to say.

Patrick kicked in the clutch and let go of the brakes and let the truck roll back a few feet. Patrick reached to unlock the truck door and he hesitated. He looked towards his grandfather lying flat in the passenger seat with his legs hanging down around the gear shift in the middle of the floorboard. Patrick pulled the back of the seat forward and reached for the crowbar lying there. He took a deep breath and held it as if he were about to dive into some water to see how long he could hold his breath. He sprang open the door, his feet hit the wet sideboard and Patrick slid straight to the ground. He rolled over and jumped to his feet with the crowbar ready to swing to fight any panther or creature that might appear. The truck lights pointed forward but gave enough light to see where the cut limbs were lying on the ground where he had removed the sawed pulpwood sticks a few hours earlier. Dead carcasses of the slaughtered panthers smelled of blood, death, gore, gasoline and truck exhaust all mixed---a smell that Patrick knew he never wanted to smell again. Nauseated and worn out, he still had adrenaline powering him forward. Looking all around, he quickly grabbed some pine limbs and stuffed them next to the back tires on the driver's side. Still looking all around, he cautiously maneuvered to the passenger's side and did the same thing. Patrick hustled back into the driver's door that he had left open to quickly get back in. He shut the door and looked over at his grandfather. Neither said anything as Patrick shifted the gear shaft and goosed the engine then with everything that the truck had. It moved inches at a time over the placed limbs, and Patrick saw a couple of the limbs fly up into the air like fleeting ghosts in the night in the muddied side mirrors as he kept moving inches at a time but moving forward, nonetheless.

"Don't stop!" His grandfather bellowed with a stronger voice.

Inch by inch the truck moved forward with its backside swaying in a side-to-side motion. Patrick was pressing the accelerator so hard that he was not even sitting in the driver's seat. He was holding the pedal all the way down to the floorboard as he grasped the steering wheel. The wheels were making a channeled path through the forest floor. Even with all the rain, the truck was moving and shaking and jolting and rattling and creating exhaust smoke that flowed like miniature clouds weaving through what was visible from the truck's headlights in the night. "What am I going to do if we get stuck again?"

"Don't get stuck. Keep going!"

Patrick was holding the steering wheel even tighter now. His foot was pushing the accelerator on the floorboard so hard that he was shaking with the motor's vibrations as if he were physically urging the truck forward. He was burning gas like he had never done before with the engine wide open. He had never felt the intense need for speed. Holding the accelerator down just inches of ground were achieved every second. The inches were reduced again until just the tires were spinning. Patrick could hear the mudslinging and feel the motor roaring, but the wet earth was winning again. Intensely Patrick gritted his teeth and hung on so tight to the steering wheel that his grandfather thought that the old truck's steering wheel might pop off at any time. His grandfather was almost paralyzed with chest pain and felt the clammy cold as if he were beginning to slip away into a fainting spell. In his mind he knew that his time on earth might not be long. He wanted desperately to help the next Keeper of the Secret, but he was all but spent.

"It's no use! We're stuck again!"

"Gun, underneath, seat."

"I forgot about it!" Patrick's voice cried out in both exhaustion and happiness.

Patrick reached for the old, double-barreled shotgun, loaded it with shells and emptied the box of shells into his pockets. He quickly opened his door and bailed out of the cab into the fading gray exhaust, headlights still beaming. This time there were cut trees directly in his headlight view, so he went straight to the limbs still holding the loaded shotgun ready for any nefarious creature or the hint of another panther. Looking all around him, he stuffed limbs under the driver's side back double tires and then started to do the same for the passenger side. One limb was the perfect size to get under the double tires, but he could not pull it free from a larger limb which penned it to the earth. Looking around into the dark he quickly stepped back to the truck and laid the shotgun on top of the hood of the truck and went quickly to pull the limb free. That's when he heard another nightmarish shriek.

More panthers were coming from the deep ravine. He could hear their paws clawing into the red dirt sides of the ravine. Oh, God, no, not a third wave, please, God, he thought. He could hear brush moving in the dark and cat cries started. He did not dare leave that gun on the hood of the truck. He dropped the limb and went running to the hood. Just as he reached the shotgun the first panther leaped forward toward Patrick into the headlights. The panther's teeth tore into Patrick's flesh as his body was pinned against the middle of the hood of the truck. With his other hand he grabbed the shotgun and was able to aim with one arm and point the barrel directly at the second panther lurking and pulled the trigger. The blast stopped the second panther and scared the first panther enough to let go, but the gun's kickback knocked Patrick's arm so hard that his shoulder felt pulled out of socket. His arm slammed against the truck knocking his shotgun from his grip. The gun slid off the hood onto the ground.

Patrick rolled off the truck's hood and instantaneously reached for the shotgun as the bloody corpse of the second panther fell at his feet and rolled underneath the truck. He pulled the double-barreled shotgun back into his grasp and was able to shoulder fire the next shot into three more panthers approaching. None were killed but all were stalled in their advance. The first panther pounced again using its cat-fanged teeth to tear into Patrick's flesh in the same bleeding injured arm. Patrick thought, "All is lost." In the intensity of the moment with maximum adrenaline flowing, he still could not pry loose from the big black cat's grip. I'm about to be ripped to shreds was all he thought as he protected his jugulars with his other arm. He heard a clang on the truck's hood as metal struck metal. The panther's eyes faded with its mouth wide open, fanged teeth exposed in order to attack his flesh again. Instantly Patrick saw a Chickasaw arrowhead emerge right above the cat's tongue. The panther fell backwards. Patrick could see an arrow had penetrated from the back of its neck into the panther's throat. The three panthers staggered by buckshot fell–one—two—three. Arrows pierced their hearts from the sides; then two new panthers approached and leaped into the air. As the black panthers, like shadows in the moonlight, were airborne in a trajectory toward Patrick, two arrows penetrated their individual heads right between their eyes. The panthers' forward motion led them right into Patrick's chest, and they knocked him back against the front fender and hood of the truck. All Patrick could see was the white foam from their mouths, snarled lips moved slowly over their vicious teeth like a curtain closing. Am I dead now or am I alive? Patrick's mental and physical exhaustion was complete. He slid to the ground. Underneath the dead panthers he gazed into the bright moonlight to see the back of a warrior Chief's long feathered headgear fleeing into the dark woods. The Chief's moving image was with just enough moonlight to see a faint but illuminated golden reflection of what Patrick had seen earlier that afternoon.

It was the chalice of gold! That's where it went! Patrick struggled to push the dead panthers away. He wanted to pursue the Chief. Was it Chief Tanglefoot? He reached down, retrieved his grandfather's shotgun, then ran and pulled back the truck door. "Pappy! Did you see him!" But there was no answer. Just his grandfather's motionless face, but his grandfather was in a sitting position looking through the windshield, with a smile on his face. Next to him on the seat was his sable tooth tiger arrowhead necklace. His eyes were open, but his skin was more than just ashen white. "Pappy! Don't die on me now. I'll get you out of here!" Patrick reached for the keys to crank the truck when he felt the first jolt. It felt as though the truck had dropped down on a roof of a large void-like chamber hollowed out beneath them with eerie vibrations, tunneled vibrations like a weird thud echoed without sound but with feeling. The truck was slipping backwards just as if its engine was cranked and in reverse. With the headlights pointing up the steep hill in the dark woods Patrick could see the trees and brush and the path where the two wheels had pressed down the brush. Then he saw the channeled ruts that he had taken so long to make moving the truck uphill inch by inch, but now the truck was moving backwards without the tires even turning. Patrick saw the stump of a tree that his grandfather had cut to make the road passable earlier that day. The truck was picking up speed in a continued reverse direction, but the wheels were still not moving. Then he saw the first tree crashing down with dirt hitting the windshield, and now all the earth was violently vibrating. He had battled the yellowjackets and the panthers and had seen the secret treasure and the Chickasaw warrior Chief and now the whole hillside was collapsing. The truck was moving without its wheels turning, falling backwards toward the deep ravine. Patrick froze. Another tree crashed hitting the truck hood and he saw his grandfather move.

"Get out! Tell your grandmother I'll see her in heaven. Go! Now! Keeper of the Secret! Go!" His grandfather slumped down again motionless, and his spent body rolled toward his passenger side door as his head rested against the glass window.

Patrick's voice was muted again. He could not express or eke out a word. In shock his hands were glued to the steering wheel. He glanced at his grandfather and then looked through the windshield to see in the truck's light beams nature's chaotic fury as trees were falling and huge chunks of the hillside were coming toward him as the truck's back wheels approached the edge of the ravine. As the cab of the truck started rising, Patrick without thinking, swung open his driver's side door and leaped toward the moving ground only to feel the entire truck turn straight up as it began its descent into the ravenous abyss. He landed on the continually moving and shaking earth. I'm about to die was all he thought as a huge pine crashed into the chaotic commotion as its flexible top pop-slapped the pulsating ground next to him.

Where was uphill now? In the brightness of the full moon dark objects were coming to him like a mudslide of rocks and trees torn from the earth with clumps of roots rolling intermixing with vines showing how they were ripped from land. Mud-like boulders and trees rolled down toward him. He jumped over a tree trunk rotating like it was in a river. He started running in the dark. No time to worry about lingering panthers he thought. He leaped over another tree trunk rolling with its unearthed roots spinning and climbed to straddle a larger trunk. Instantly Patrick felt a strong tug on his left arm. "Keeper of the Secret, follow me!"

It was Chief Tanglefoot!

Chief Tanglefoot ran up the fallen top of a tree's trunk till he met the flared-out roots and then jumped across to another fallen tree top and never lost a beat in the ensuing chaos. Patrick followed his steps panting in disbelief and in full distress. Patrick then slipped and hollered out as his feet slid off a tree trunk. He straddled the moving trunk in its downward movement. Chief

Tanglefoot stopped, jumped back and stretched out his one huge free hand. Patrick could see the golden chalice in his other hand. Then he grabbed his hand, and the Chief pulled him up as if he were a turkey feather. Once again, they both ran up more fallen trees like two salmon swimming upstream against the currents trying to get back home. Chief Tanglefoot ran on his bare toes like a gazelle as if going up multiple down escalators in a flawless jump and cross timing pattern. Branches were snapping, thuds of crashing trees still filled the air, and the gross sucking sound of Mississippi clay pulled apart in house-sized globs as the entire side of the ridge slid into the ravine and filled it up. Then in the midst of the swirling chaos and debris-moving fiasco, just as they ran up the last tree trunk that had fallen, they faced a steep twenty foot newly made cliff of mud. Chief Tanglefoot didn't say a word but pointed with the golden chalice toward a fallen tree. He raced there with his bare feet in the sucking fresh clay exposed during the earthquake and mudslide. Patrick's boots stuck into the gooky clay, and he couldn't move. "Chief Tanglefoot!" The Chief turned and without missing a beat he reached out his arm and lifted Patrick straight into the air as his boots remained in the mirey clay. Barefooted like the Chief, Patrick followed him to the tree, once again with its trunk lying against the edge of the cliff and its top resting in the exposed clay. He watched Chief Tanglefoot wrap the gold cup around his waist with a rope and then the chief started climbing up using the branches of the large pine as a ladder. Patrick copied the chief but advanced upward slower. As they reached the top of the ridge, the shaking stopped, and the earth finally stood still, and the grotesque sounds of goopy clay and sandstones rolling and brush and branches meshing into the ground ceased. Now the entire woods that had covered the downhill descent were missing. A full moon peacefully reflected the sun's rays onto this land. Patrick was out of breath, his chest heaving for oxygen. He was ready to spill himself into this ridge dirt face first and kiss the very sand that had healed the yellowjacket stings just hours earlier. He looked to see Chief Tanglefoot, but the Chief was nowhere to be seen. Disappeared. His grandfather and the secret of the ancient Indians were now buried deeper and more secured than ever before. Chief Tanglefoot was gone. The new Keeper of the Secret was alone.

S O U T H
P A C I F I C
O C E A N

hatchiebooks.com

Pontiac.

De Soto

www.ingramcontent.com/pod-product-compliance
Lightning Source LLC
LaVergne TN
LVHW041103150826
845673LV00007B/1899

* 9 7 9 8 2 1 8 2 3 8 3 8 4 *